COCKY
SOLDIER

FALEENA HOPKINS

Cocky Soldier

Cover Image licensed from Shutterstock.com
Cover Designed by Faleena Hopkins
Published by Hop Hop Publications

ISBN-13: 978-1542552035
ISBN-10: 1542552036

Love is like war:
easy to begin but very
hard to stop.

H. L. Mencken

1

MEAGAN

Something is sniffing my fingers. Where the hell am I? Okay, not scary at all, but I'm blinking at a black, huge, beast of a dog with tan markings, larger than any I've ever seen before. He's less than a foot away from my face. He's stepping backwards like he didn't think his dinner would wake up, and that gives me a greater view of a living room with virtually nothing in it in terms of furniture. Bryan's mansion doesn't have that creepy curtain-less window. My head is pounding. Why does my face feel crusty in places, wet in others?

If I'm at a spa in a facial mask they really need to spruce up their vibe. Add some Enya crooning in the background instead of that deep, male voice talking to someone other than me. Wait. I'm not alone.

"Where am I?!" I scream, sitting up like a shot.

Leaping in front of me—one hand out, the other holding a phone to his ear—is a shirtless guy so handsome that upon sight of him my open mouth clamps shut. His naked chest is sculpted, olive skin shadowed in all the right places, and there's a tattoo of spindly lines and the letter *C* carved into the top of his left pectoral muscle. But there's red stuff on his perfect chest that looks like blood!

He gives an address into the phone and mutters, eyeing me, "She's awake."

"Yeah! I'm awake!" I croak, glancing behind me to see if he's alone. "Did I ruin your evil plan?"

Back there is a sliver of a bare kitchen through a cracked-open door.

And that closed door to my right might lead to a coat closet…or to a basement where this guy keeps all his victims. The dog is between me and the front door.

In this bare bones room is a coffee table and a ratty chair. No art. White walls with scuff marks. A beat-up bicycle, tires inflated. Maybe that's how he gets here. This couch is older than my grandfather's grandpa's mother. Just ahead awaits a hallway leading to other crappy places I never want to see.

None of it fits in with how intensely handsome and seemingly normal this guy looks. This is not just some bachelor pad. It doesn't even look lived in.

Which means I'm in trouble.

He must be coo-coo-for-Cocoa-Puffs crazy.

This isn't where he lives.

It's where he stashes us.

"Tell whoever the fuck you're talking to that you picked the wrong girl to kidnap! I know self-defense, asshole!" Jumping off the couch I kick at his knees to topple his abducting ass to the ground, but he jumps backward out of reach. No, he didn't *jump*, exactly. He glided without effort as though he's had training of his own, dark-chocolate eyes sharpening in an instant.

And now I'm on the ground. Nice. The hound from hell makes a sound like it's embarrassed for me and we lock eyes. As I moan under the weight of the pain in my skull, its ears cock back on a head tilt.

"Calm down!" the guy orders me. "You need to be careful."

My eyes shoot up and meet his. "Says the kidnapper."

He frowns into the phone, "Hurry. Her head's not on right. She's combative." After a pause, he mutters, "No, I'm not worried about that. I can handle her. I've dealt with worse. I'll be waiting." He hangs up and tucks the phone into his sweats' pocket.

"You've dealt with *worse*? You get off on it or something? Huh?! HUH?! Good-looking guy like you can get any girl he wants so instead he *steals* and tortures them? Does that make you hot, sick fucker?!"

I try to kick at him again, but he backs up and sighs, crossing his arms, which makes his biceps spread out and look enormously strong. I stare at them thinking I might not be able to overtake him after all. I lied about the self-defense. I've been meaning to take classes. And right now I wish to God I hadn't put that off.

He leans down and engages my stare. "I didn't '*steal*' you. Get back on the couch and stop trying to attack me. I'm not the enemy, and you have a concussion."

Stunned, my hand floats to my head, and horror waves into me. "Is this my own blood?"

"Yes."

Real fear takes hold—all bravado gone. "Okay, please don't hurt me," I whisper.

"I'm not going to hurt you, you freak! You drove into a tree. I had to get you to a phone. Couldn't leave you out in the cold bleeding like that. An ambulance is on its way. Now, just calm the fuck down."

We stare at each other while he tilts his stunning head, waiting for me to catch on.

"You actually *live* here?"

"Yes," he mutters, annoyed. "And you almost hit me and my dog."

10

My reckless driving quickly jumps up and replays in my wounded, delusional mind like a game of charades. Three syllables. Car accident. Wait, that's four. Whatever. Suddenly it all makes sense to me.

2

MEAGAN

Seventeen minutes ago.

If I blow through this red light, what's the worst that could happen?

The guy who invented snooze buttons needs to be punched out cold and when he wakes up nine minutes later, punched out again. I'll do the honors, shouting after round three, "How does it feel?! Refreshed?!"

I think it's safe to run this.

No cops to my left or my right.

There's a single, blue Kia with a busted muffler and one broken taillight, which I can see only because it's buzzing away from me. He doesn't care if I break the law. Other than him, 14th Street is empty.

As the morning sky inches toward a lighter shade of grey, there's nobody to witness this illegal move save for totally screwed, late-for-work, little ole me.

What time is it?

5:55 A.M.

No problem. I can make it there by six.

If someone invented time travel and I went back eighteen minutes.

Dammit!

I hate being late. Every morning.

"Just floor it, Meagan. No one's gonna know."

Slamming the gas pedal with my stylish boot I smoke the red and launch into a residential area. Can't afford to pay for another speeding ticket just because my boss is an unforgiving genius and I'm afraid of losing my job, so I give a quick glance over my shoulder to make damn sure the rearview mirror wasn't lying. No cops. Fuck yeah! I'm the luckiest rebel on the planet.

I whip back around to face front.

My eyes snap open wide as they can get. One of those ridiculously large speed bumps they randomly install in residential neighborhoods has materialized before me.

Too late. Can't slow. Here I go!

My hot pink Prius catches air like it never has—or ever should. The front wheels crash onto the pavement first. The rear two catch up a million feet later. I whoop with rebellious joy followed by a peal of laughter that most people pay good money for and have to shove into a bong to get.

I have personally kept my guardian angel solidly employed for every single one of my twenty-five years. I'm surprised she hasn't quit, but she's still with me, so here I am, ripping a good 55 MPH in a 25 MPH zone, loving every second of it.

This character flaw drives my mother crazy.

She says that because I am young I believe I will live for eternity. I don't believe I'll live forever. I know I will. Not in this flesh, but in some dish I have yet to create that people will share the recipe of for centuries to come. That's the goal.

With Beethoven's 'Ode to Joy' blasting my eardrums to bits from speakers that can *barely* handle the pain, I grin like crazy. Even if I'm late to Bryan's house, what an adventure this morning has been so far!

It'll be worth the ass chewing I'm in for. He's going to growl and threaten to fire me, but he won't follow through with it.

I kinda wish he would.

And I kinda wish he wouldn't.

Because I kinda have a crush on him.

Okay…I very much have a crush on my boss, and we're kinda sleeping together.

Most talented chefs are extremely hard to deal with, so I'm fine with him being a total dick at times. There have been many when I wanted to quit, slap him, or both, and not in that order. But then there are those dreamy blue eyes and that amazingly confident smile that both stop me from doing anything but whatever he says.

He's charismatic, as many egotistical people are. So full of himself that you want to be full of him, too. Pun intended.

What time is it?

6:01 A.M.

I am officially one inexcusable minute late.

Dammit, my phone is vibrating.

I mutter, reaching for my cell, "Was he sitting there watching the clock?!"

In my reach I accidentally turn the wheel to the left. Not much. Just a little. Unfortunately, in the swerve, my phone slides right off the passenger seat and onto the floor, still ringing, his name ominously glowing from the screen: *Bryan Marchand.*

"Hang on. I'm coming," I mutter, leaning down to reach. My cell slides further to the right, nestling in the corner of the floor among the ignored lint and dead leaf fragments. I grunt, "Get over here you stupid phone," and stretch my right arm as far as it can go while my left steers with no one behind the wheel.

The very tips of my fingers finally touch plastic. Just a little farther! Reach, reach, and, "Gotcha!"

Bryan's name disappears.

"Fuck! I missed it."

He's been sent to voicemail, which he'll hate.

Groaning I straighten up, look out the windshield, and scream.

I'm speeding toward a stop sign.

On the other side of the street.

There's a jogger.

He's got a dog.

They're heading for the crosswalk.

I'm going to hit them.

He and I lock eyes.

Turn the wheel, Meagan!

3

JEREMY

"No, buddy. We're sleeping in today," I mumble into the pillow.

Instead of curling back up on the ratty rug by my bed, Aslan continues staring at me with the kind of persistence I'm not in the mood for. The mattress sinks under his furry chin as he doubles the effort with sad eyes.

"C'mon, buddy," I grumble. "We always get up early."

He thumps his heavy paw on the bed.

"Just one morning, can I sleep in?!"

He thumps again.

I roll over so I don't have to look at him. "Give me one more hour!"

Rottweilers, as a breed, talk, so he lets me know what he thinks of my procrastination by a short howl so fucking unignorable that I have to throw my legs over the side of the bed and stand, rubbing my eyes while shaking my head to clear out the dust.

17

"Fine. I'm up. Better than having that dream again," I grumble.

I slept like I was back in Fallujah, not here in Atlanta, Georgia, the city I was raised in.

In other words, I slept like shit.

Panting with happiness, Aslan's nubby tail bobs back and forth. He backs up to give me room while I drag navy blue sweats up my legs, slam a matching blue hoodie on my torso.

"Did you know I was havin' a nightmare? That why you woke me, boy?"

I give his super soft, huge head a pat, then shove sneakers on my bare feet, forgetting all about socks. The house keys get swiped off my rickety coffee table along with his leash that I fasten around his collar in less than a heartbeat of time. As soon as we clear the front door we're off and running, leaving the single-story, one-bedroom, house I bought when I got out of the Marines in our wake.

Every slap of my soles against the sidewalk, every intake of fresh morning air in my lungs, and the past steadily loses its grip on my psyche.

Aslan's gait matches my rhythmic pace and I glance to him, take in his happy, carefree concentration and wildly flapping tongue. God...so lucky I found him. Without this guy I'd be in bed until dinner every damn day.

He needs these runs, sure.

Every dog does.

But I think my buddy knows I need them, too.

I didn't want to wake up, but now that I'm running I feel better. Relieved. Ghosts are left behind me. Just me and my dog and the blissful silence of dawn. My home is in a quiet neighborhood, a deliberate choice. At this hour the streets are always empty.

If I lived in a busy neighborhood I'd be tense from all the unexpected noises.

I'd be searching for an oncoming fight that never comes anymore.

Silence is necessary to my sanity.

But what I don't need is a Prius so quiet I can't hear it coming.

My eyes lock with the driver's. She's headed right for us.

Adrenaline shoots into me like I've been punched.

I yank Aslan's leash back.

His paws struggle to run backwards, the fur around his neck stretched under his chain-collar.

The girl's hands dig into the steering wheel, turning to the right.

Her car skids away just in time, so close that wind touches my face like a whisper from The Reaper.

But she's not so lucky.

With that quick turn she over-corrected and I shout as she crashes right into the oak tree on the corner, the one diagonal from where Aslan and I stand. She wraps right around the damn thing like her car is made of tin.

Everything goes silent again. Except in my own fucked up head. Rifles explode as I race to the wreck. I know they're not real, just a mirage from my memories I might never be able to shake.

Put Jeremy Cocker on the front lines.

He's the quickest to react.

Jeremy was made to fight.

He's never scared.

Yeah, right. I'm scared all the time, like everybody.

I just ignore it.

I make it to the crumpled hunk of metal and yank on the locked door handle, scanning her bloody face like a robot calculating data. The airbag is splattered liquid red and ballooned around her. I shout through the glass. "Hey! You alive?!"

She doesn't answer, eyes closed, lips parted.

"Aslan, go there!" I shout and point him to the sidewalk. Pulling off my hoodie, I wrap the thick cotton around my right arm and slam my elbow through the driver's side rear window, glass shattering. Reaching over shards of it

I unlock the driver's door and rush to yank it open and lift her out of the car.

I've gotta call an ambulance.

Cops, too.

They'll need a report.

The car is totaled.

Left my cell phone at home. Hell, I hardly use the thing, so of course I don't have it with me. "Aslan, come!"

As we rush back, his leash dragging unmanned, I keep checking on her and repeating, "Hang in there. Don't die on me," but the sight of her bloody in my arms is jarring. I grit my teeth and shut the ghosts out. Jesus, how many times have I carried the wounded?

Too many.

4

MEAGAN

Back to present time.

Slinking up onto the couch, all I can manage is an embarrassed, "Oh. Oops. With how this place looks I thought…"

He cocks an eyebrow, waiting for me to finish insulting him.

I blink in shock, thrust my arm out and croak, "Oh my God!" and he relaxes a little. "I have to go. Bryan's going to kill me!" Jumping up and forgetting all about the concussion, I swing the guy's front door open, absolutely horrified by what's outside. Groaning, I mourn, "It's fully daylight? How long have I been here? Dawn is over. What time is it? Bryan must be losing his mind. Uh-oh…whoa."

Naked muscles wrap around me before I hit the welcome mat. I'm carried back to the couch while he murmurs, "Okay, that's enough. The only place you're going to is the hospital." As an aside he grumbles, "And here I thought you were saying, *Oh my God,* because you almost hit us, not because you're afraid of letting down your stupid boyfriend."

My mind isn't normal. It hasn't been for months since Bryan and I started hooking up. He's so much older than me and can play the 'game' so much better. Maybe because I don't want to play any games at all. I'm confused. Maybe it is the head-injury. Whatever the reason, while I'm being laid on the couch by this total stranger who I just thought might be a kidnapper, I confess, "He's not my boyfriend. He's a god."

"Oh he is, huh?"

"And you don't anger the gods."

Dude cocks a gorgeous eyebrow. "Whatever. Just stay here." He disappears down the hallway and returns with a blanket, laying it over me before he heads for the kitchen. Time is playing tricks on me because suddenly a glass of water is being shoved in my face. "Drink this. It's not poisoned. Just good, clean, drinking water."

He kneels down and I sip while he holds the glass. "Thank you." I lick my lips and mutter, "Who are you?"

Like he doesn't want to tell me personal details about himself, he glares at me. I think I've pissed him off. Huge wall around his eyes. Maybe I shouldn't have made the comment about his home.

So I sheepishly offer, "I'm sorry I thought you were a kidnapper. Now, who are you?"

He dryly mutters, "Not a god, that's who I am."

"Well, I know that!" I cry out like someone drunk. "What's your name, human?"

His full lips twitch. "I'm Jeremy Cocker."

"Like the singer, *Joe* Cocker?"

"If that sticks into your foggy brain, sure."

"Are you related to him?"

"No."

"Why not?"

He blinks like I'm an idiot. "Because I'm not. Who're *you*, human? What's *your* name?"

Footsteps approaching from outside pull his focus because the front door is still open. He rises up, each awe-inspiring inch of his insanely sculpted body sliding into vision a mere foot away from my eyes, ending with his crotch. "She's in here!" he calls out. My fingers reach for the strings on his sweats and he swats my hands away. "Jesus," he mutters.

My head lolls back and I meet his eyes. "Sorry. Primal instinct."

Two determined EMTs appear next to him, one male and one female. Normal looking people, not like you see on television. All work and no play, they start locking down the legs of a rolling gurney. The female asks, "How's your back? Your neck?"

"Not broken. And I don't need that. I can walk."

With authority Jeremy Cocker informs them, "No, she can't."

"I can!"

"She tried to take off, and bit dirt."

This solidifies their sense of purpose. They completely ignore my repeated objections and lift me onto it while I glare at Jeremy. "I'm Meagan Forrester."

"Charmed, I'm sure," he mutters and turns to the policeman who just walked in. "Did you see the car?"

The mustached cop answers with a superior nod, "We drove past the scene on our way here. Now, why don't you tell me what happened?"

As the gurney gently bounces me out of the house toward the ambulance I listen to Jeremy lying through his perfect teeth, "My dog saw a squirrel. Lunged into the crosswalk. She thought she was gonna hit him, turned the wheel too hard."

Why'd he lie for me? I'm not complaining. A hiked insurance premium I do not want. Not exactly swimming in green backs since I bought my condo. Then I hear him finish the lie with, "You know how girls are."

The police officer says, "They can't drive for shit."

The two men walk out of the house as Jeremy agrees, "Exactly."

Lifting my pounding head so I look them in the eyes, I shout, "I can drive just fine!"

Jeremy smirks and shouts back, "Says the girl being carried to the hospital!"

"I'm an excellent driver, you jerk! And I can walk on my own!"

I try to climb off the gurney but one of the EMTs warns me, "No no no. Take it easy. A concussion is not—"

" —Don't tell me to be calm!" Clamoring down like a marionette who's got a child holding its strings, I don't succeed. The white hospital blanket tangles around my legs and I fall in a heap of awkward. Worst part is the world spins in a slow, nauseating circle like I'm underwater, submerged in a sea of my own embarrassment.

Two pairs of hands lift me up, one of them Jeremy's. He mutters, "Nice one, Grace."

"It's Meagan!"

"I know."

"My head's not on right!" The EMTs force me into the ambulance and I stop the struggle, but turn to point at Jeremy. "I don't like you."

He waves at me until the door closes.

And off we go.

"Go faster. Turn the horns on. Get me away from that guy."

Sitting on a chair by my side while we bounce and sway with the vehicle's increasing speed the female EMT smiles to herself. "I don't know why you'd want to get away from him." She reaches for medical gadgets and eyes me from profile. "He's one of the Cocker Brothers."

"He said he wasn't related to Joe Cocker! God, he lies about everything!"

The male EMT calls back from behind the wheel, "Joe Cocker was British. Performed at Woodstock. No relation. He died in 2014."

"Oh," I mutter.

She checks my blood pressure, wrapping my arm, strapping the velcro and pumping away until it's like my arm is sucked dry by a python. "You don't know about the Cocker Brothers? Are you from here?"

Now I'm annoyed mixed with defensive. We who are natives of the ATL are very loyal to our city. "Born and raised! Why? Who are they?"

"Six of the most gorgeous men in town, each as hot as the last depending on your flavor." She glances down to read the numbers, satisfied I'm not going to die.

The male EMT sarcastically calls back, "Your flavor? What are they, scoops of ice cream?"

She smirks, "Better," clearly thinking dirty things.

He shifts in his seat, turns on the radio and grumbles, "Nothing special about any of 'em!"

She whispers to me, really quietly so he can't hear, "The men may not like them, but the women sure do." She didn't actually wink but she might as well have. "If I weren't married, I would've asked Mark there to take you to Emergency all by himself so I could stay back there, take my shot. My younger sister used to have a crush on Jeremy in high school. He's all grown up now. Fair game."

"What are you whispering about, Sheila?"

"Nothing," she calls up to Mark.

In desperate need of pain medication, I couldn't care less about what she's saying, so I close my eyes and mutter, "Whoever Jeremy Cocker is, he's no Bryan Marchand."

5

JEREMY

A beer-gutted tow-truck driver is waiting at the wheel of his humming vehicle, parking behind the smashed, hot pink, tin can.

With familiarity they nod to each other.

"Bob," the cop greets him.

"Hey Sam," the driver smiles. His door creaks open and old work boots slap the ground.

I'm here to explain the story again, and get this cop out of here as quick as I can. Officer Sam is a piece of work, one of those pricks who joined the force to have legal power over civilians. I've seen his kind before, in the Marines. Thank God they're rare.

"So you were on that corner?" He motions to it with his chin.

"Yeah, and the squirrel headed across the street this way." I point out the imaginary squirrel's journey. "Aslan

29

wanted to chase it up that tree. We were in the street at the beginning of the crosswalk here. I didn't want him going after the squirrel so I yanked his leash, but Meagan thought she was going to hit him, turned her wheel hard and then bam. This happened."

"So when the dog couldn't chase the squirrel, the girl decided to give it a shot," he dryly jokes, throwing me a look that says, *we're both in on the private gag called women-are-beneath-us*.

I nod to play along. Fact is I pegged this cop's true nature the second I saw him. There was an evil glint in his eyes that I'd seen before. It's now become my job to keep Meagan safe. By the way he was looking at her on the couch, I knew he'd try and have a go at her.

She's got the same shade of warm brown hair and caramel eyes as Natalie Portman, with a heart-shaped face like hers, too. None of the aloofness though. Pretty funny, too, and she's got a fight to her.

Meagan was the perfect candidate for stalking by a shady cop like Officer Sam. I've got nothing against authority except when it's abused.

During boot camp my observation skills became so sharply honed I can read most people before they speak. As soon as I got there I'd kept my mouth shut and stuck out the loneliness of being away from the family I'd always been so close to, especially my brother Jake. We were roommates until I decided to enlist and we were inseparable. That was part of the problem.

There I was with a bunch of strangers, all of us put through the most rigorous training a person can receive. I was quiet a lot. A little lost. I watched people. Learned to trust myself when my instincts proved accurate time and again. And it's a good thing. When we got deployed I was careful around the locals we had to live amongst in countries that didn't want Americans around. The skill at judging people and trusting my instincts kept me alive.

That, and luck.

"Looks like she should leave squirrel-chasing to the dogs," I smirk, hiding that I want this over with.

Tow-Truck Bob takes the keys from her ignition and calls over his thick shoulder, "What should I do with her purse?"

My lie tumbles out as casually as if it were true. "I said I'd return it to her. Her house keys, too."

"I'll just keep the fob."

He tears it off the ring and hands them over with the phone, and a purse so heavy I mutter, "Jesus, what's in here? Maryland?"

Officer Sam informs me, "I need her phone." My eyebrows twitch like I don't get it. His face gets severe as he explains, "Need to get her phone number off it so I can call her for the report."

"Oh, right. Hang on." I pretend to click it open, hiding the screen from his line of vision. "Fuck. Sorry. It's got a password lock on it." I stuff it into the bag next to the lamp, sofa, and live giraffe. "But I'll make sure she calls the station to give the report."

His eyes narrow. "You friends with her?"

"With Meagan? Hell yeah."

"Thought she introduced herself to you back there."

I chuckle, "Oh, when I said, *Charmed I'm sure?* I said that because I've known her forever. Friends since Confirmation class. She just bumped her head pretty badly. I'll call her parents when I get back. Let 'em know she's okay."

His suspicious eyes go dead. Can't argue in the face of Catholicism. He turns to Tow-Truck Bob like I just ruined his weekend plans. "How long?"

"Few minutes, Sam. Gotta jimmy the thing off of this tree."

"You need anything else from me?" I ask, friendly as can be. "I can stick around. Help you get it on the truck."

Glad to be rid of me he waves his nasty fingers. "Nah, Go on. Git."

"Thank you, Officer."

"Wait up!"

I glance back and see him holding out a card. "Have her call me to give a report."

Wow, this guy's stubborn.

I walk over, taking the diseased slip of paper like I'm impressed. She'll never get this card. Ever. "I'll give it to her, first thing. Have a good one. Gotta go walk my dog. He never got a chance to do his business."

I tip my head to both of them, then break into a jog, the purse gripped in my fist. As soon as I'm near enough for Aslan to hear me I shout, "I'm comin' buddy!"

He lets out one of those howl-yelps, which instantly makes me feel bad for him. Breaking into a sprint I whip open the door and let him out to sniff the front lawn for the perfect spot.

I shouldn't be sifting through Meagan's things…but I'm only human.

Three lipsticks that all look the same.

Wait, no. Different names. Berry's Burden. Nude Pleasure. Lilac Lover.

"What the fuck," I mutter, tossing them back inside.

A pair of sneakers wrapped in a plastic bag. Probably for the gym. Yep, here's a gym bra.

Two magazines — Bon Appétit and Gourmet.

Three cooking ladles.

One spatula.

Loose coins.

Travel toothbrush. Toothpaste. Sample bottle of Listerine. Waxed dental floss, its lettering rubbed off by wear.

"Girl's got a thing for oral hygiene."

I open up her wallet, hot pink just like her car, while continuing to talk to myself as I figure her out. "License. Meagan Leigh Forrester. Twenty-five-years-old. Lives around the corner if this is accurate. A couple well-used credit cards. Triple-A Roadside Assistance membership card. Could've used that one today, huh, Meagan? What's this? Half of a paper, one-dollar bill? Who's got the other half? Family member? Bryan the god? Ho ho ho, what's this? Your business card?"

Turning it over reveals that it's not hers. It's Bryan Marchand's. As soon as I gather he's a bigwig chef her phone rings and guess who it is.

6

JEREMY

Without hesitation I swipe to answer, "Hello?"

The guy's volume nearly blows my ear off. "Where the hell have you been?! I've been calling you for over an hour!"

"Sorry, dude. I don't swing that way."

He pauses. "Who the hell is this?!"

Aslan lumbers into the house, happier and lighter now. I kick my front door shut after him, thinking I'm in need of some fun. Smirking, I ask Bryan Marchand, "You want to know who I am?"

"Yes!"

"Me?"

"Yes, you!"

"You want to know who I am."

"Goddammit! Yes! Who the fuck are you and why are you answering Meagan's phone?"

"I'm her lover."

"What?"

"Her boy toy. Her sex pooch. Her slave. But only on Wednesdays. She won't give me more than that."

"What?!"

"Wait, are you her *Fridays,* you lucky bastard? Because if you are you're two days early. Sorry, I've got dibs today. Check your calendar."

Dead silence on the other end of the line for a whole three seconds.

"Don't you dare *fucking* tell me she's in your bed, whoever the fuck you are, when she's supposed to be *at work!*"

Shoving my index finger in my ear and wiggling so I can get my hearing back, I mutter with believable innocence, "Oh shit. This is her boss? God, sorry, man. Yeah, she's passed out from all the hot sex."

"Get her on the phone!"

"She said to tell you she's busy."

"She WHAT?!"

With a grin I head into the kitchen to brew a much-needed cup of coffee. "She's busy." He starts swearing like a sailor after his boat sank with booze in it. When he quiets I dryly ask, "You done?"

"Yes."

I chuckle, "I'm kidding, Bryan! She's not here. She was

in a car accident. She's at the hospital. I'm the guy she almost hit. They took her away in an ambulance and the cop gave me her purse to return to her. I'm just fucking with you because you shouldn't talk to a lady that way. So calm down and go make sure she's okay."

Another silence. "You were fucking with me."

"I was."

"She's hurt?"

"Yes."

"How bad is it?"

"Hit her head. Concussion, I think. Will need some time off. With pay."

"Fuck that!" he explodes. "If she misses my grand opening this Saturday I will—"

He hangs up, threat hovering in the air undefined.

"What a dick," I mutter, staring at the phone.

I decide to poke around.

I won't dig too deep.

Eh, maybe I will. We'll see.

In the texts window, his thread is at the top. Aside from the slew of texts this morning demanding to know where she is, I focus mostly on his side of the convo on previous days.

You fucked up again. What do I pay you for?

When I say to order truffle oil, you order truffle oil. Stop asking me what kind and take some fucking initiative!

My lawyer emailed and you didn't tell me immediately? Did your parents drop you as a child?

"Jesus, I want to punch this guy in the neck," I mutter, reading on until…

That red blouse you wore today? Wear it again. Tomorrow. No bra.

My eyebrows fly up.

The wink-emoticon she replied with makes me chuckle to my dog, "Aslan, she's not seriously dating this asshole is she?"

Sliding the phone in my pocket I hit the single cup brew button on my functional, low-frills coffee maker and lean against the counter.

I don't get it.

How the fuck does a smart girl like that, with her fight and courage, end up with a jerk who talks to her that way? Two seconds after she opened her eyes I clocked her as being smarter than half of society. But she lets him treat her like she's beneath him, stupid, and incompetent.

I want to see his face.

See what a god looks like in the flesh.

I'm curious.

Aslan's toenails tap tap tap their way into the kitchen and I bend over to give him a good rub down before he lies down, eyes on me.

Grabbing my sole coffee mug from where I left it to dry on a ratty hand towel by the sink, I lock eyes with my dog. "Hey Aslan…you thinking what I'm thinking?"

His ears go back, head cocked.

7

MEAGAN

After discovering me sitting in the packed emergency waiting room, disconsolate and bandaged, my worried older sister shakes rain off her hair and asks, "See why I made you memorize my number? You called me old fashioned but when you lose your phone it comes in handy doesn't it?"

Rolling my eyes with a half-smile I say, "Why don't you just do a dance and sing *I told you so,* while you're at it? You were right, okay? But I don't want to hear it right now. I've been poked at, X-rayed, patched up, and I just want to get out of here, call Bryan, and find out what happened to my car."

Cecily pokes at the gauze on my head, brown eyebrows furrowed. "Can I see?" She lifts up the tape and makes a face, deep-caramel eyes locking onto mine. We could be twins if we weren't seven years apart and she didn't still have the baby weight. "Stitches! God, they look awful."

"Let's hope I get a scar."

"*Only you* would want one."

"Makes me more interesting," I shrug, heading for the door with her and batting my eyelashes for her help.

"What do you want?" she groans.

"Will you call Bryan for me? It would cushion the blow if you were the one who told him how hurt I am. He can't yell at you. He doesn't yell at other people. Except me and the other chefs."

We step onto the mats triggering the automatic-door sensors. They whoosh open, whipping our hair back with the wind, loud rainfall dancing into our ears.

She glances to me from the corners of her eyes, trying to understand why I'm dating this guy. *Dating* being a very loose term. "Meagan."

"Oh, come on. Don't judge. Remember Steve?"

She loses the judgmental face immediately. We all have a guy in our past who *owned* us. Where we did things we shouldn't have. And hey, sometimes it works out? Right?

"Cecily, he's going to be *so* pissed at me. But if you call, like you did when I was in grade school and Mom wouldn't, then maybe he'll go easy on me. We have a shot. I need you. Please try." More batting of the eyelashes before I glance to her hands, which are empty, save for her SUV key fob. "You didn't bring an umbrella?"

Sighing she explains, "It broke after ten good, loyal years. And every time I go to the store to buy a new one I get distracted by Kevin, buy a bunch of other stuff with him squirming in the cart, and then when I'm on my way home, guess what?"

"You remember that you forgot to buy the umbrella."

Throwing her hands up she cries out, "I've already put Kevin in the car seat, he's stopped squirming, so am I going to turn around and go back at that point?"

"No," I flatly answer, knowing her.

"No! I just promise myself I'll put a note on the fridge to buy one next time I'm at Target or the mall, or anywhere, because Lord knows they sell them all over Atlanta, but do I have an umbrella in my hands? No. They're everywhere but right here." She holds up her almost empty fingers as thunder cracks through the air. We both glance to the sky from under this awning where it's nice and dry, and back to each other. "Ready to get wet?"

"Do I have a choice?"

"I have baby brain!"

"I thought that's just when you're pregnant."

"Turns out it's when they're two-years-old, too. Let's hurry!"

Forgetting I've got a head wound we take off running, but my noggin starts pounding.

I shout over the downpour, "I can't!"

She stops and blinks at me with rain on her eyelashes. "Get back under the canopy! I'll come get you!"

Running with my hand shielding the already soaking wet gauze I mutter under my breath. "Dammit." I was supposed to design reminder email invitations for Le Marchand's pre-grand opening this Saturday, call the food suppliers, who haven't gotten back to us, make sure the plumber showed up at the restaurant, and twenty thousand other tasks he pays me well to take care of so he can be the genius that he is.

I'm good at multi-tasking. I'm good at my job. No matter what he says. It's why he keeps me around. Plus I know he cares about me, and that's why he's so volatile. You should see him in the kitchen, always shouting and tearing his gorgeous hair out. And holy fuck the obscenities! But that's how I don't take the abuse to heart...too much. He loves kitchens more than any other place, thing, or person in the world, and he always loses his shit there. So when he explodes at me, I take it as a compliment. Plus, since I'm just his apprentice, his yelling like he does at the chefs, makes me feel like one, too. So it almost feels good.

Her Subaru comes to an abrupt halt in front of the Emergency Room entrance where I'm tapping my feet with impatience. She waves me over, leaning down to watch me like the roof of her car just lost ten inches of space.

Climbing in I tell her, "My gauze is useless."

"You want them to put a new one on?"

"Don't make me go back in there."

"It's okay. I have some. Don't worry." Peering out the windshield she slowly drives into the storm. "When we learned we were going to have a boy Mike went overboard with the First Aid stuff. He and his brother were always breaking bones, cutting themselves open. And you remember how Devin was." She meets my eyes and I glance away to the windshield. Inhaling deeply she adds under her breath, "Knew we were in for a ride."

"I'm feeling bad enough as it is, Cess. Why'd you have to bring up Devin?"

"Sorry."

I hit the heated seat button and settle in, staring out at the raindrops, stomach tense. My mind travels back to a safer place, to my daily obsession—my boss and occasional lover.

"When did you know that Mike was the one?"

"I still don't know," she shrugs.

I stare at her in shock. "Are you serious?"

While focusing on the road she explains, "I don't believe in a soul mate, Meagan, never have. You're the romantic in the family, you know that."

Snorting I mutter, "Not anymore. No romantics left."

She doesn't argue. Mom and Dad are still together but for years now they've just been going through the motions. Roommates, not romantic partners. They don't even sleep in the same bed since Mom snores and won't wear one of those nose thingies. Cecily and I secretly suspect she adores her private space so she can read her romance novels without him grumbling for her to turn the light off.

"I don't know, is there just one person meant for us? Maybe…maybe not. But what if my guy lives in India and I'll never be truly happy because he's afraid of flying and will die over there, never having met me? Me all the way over here in America? Can you imagine how fucked up that would be? I can't believe that. I think we could be really happy with a lot of people. There are *billions* running around on the planet, and sure, many you're not attracted to, but many you are. Find one that makes you happy then love them until you both drop."

We drive on in silence, with me wondering if Bryan would make me happy. No one at the restaurant has been aware during the staff's training and Bryan and I solidifying all the intricate details, that our working relationship is peppered with the occasional illicit and very naked evening. Nobody knows about that tasty little secret, so I can't claim aloud that we're together. Or even whisper it.

But does he make me happy?

Would he, if things became serious?

God, I can't wait for his restaurant to open, when I'll be cooking alongside him. Learning from a master.

I. Can't. Wait.

As she pulls into the driveway of her two-story home set cozily in a nook beside Midtown, I reach over and touch my sister's forearm. "I need one more question answered before we go inside."

Engaging the emergency brake she turns to me. "Yes?"

"Are you happy with Mike?"

A smile spreads. "So happy. And he's so great with Kevin, such a great father. But is he my soulmate?" She leans toward me with adorable mischief in her eyes. "Maybe!"

We jump out and dash through the downpour into the house where my brother-in-law is standing in the living room, watching CNN, my two-year-old nephew in his arms. "Hey babe," he smiles to his wife, and then bobs his chin at me. "You okay, Meagan?"

"I'll be fine. They gave me a bunch of instructions but what I really need is a new bandage."

"It's really comin' down out there, huh?"

"What else is new?"

Cecily kisses Mike and then her son, grinning at him. "Hey big guy. Momma's home." He gives her a huge smile and holds out his arms. "Stay with Daddy a second. I need to help Aunt Meagan." She calls over her shoulder, as she heads to the upstairs bathroom. "Have to get the First Aid kit. Be right back."

Baby Kevin's eyes are locked on his momma, so I capture his attention by wiggling my fingers around and making funny noises. He gives me a smile, and I glance to Mike to ask, "Do you have soda water? My stomach is queasy."

"Sure, take him."

With my nephew on my hip I head for the guest bathroom to get a couple towels. "How ya been, baby boy? I missed you!" He gazes at me, soaking in every detail of my face with a child's silent curiosity. "I'm diggin' how you're styling your hair. Is that a new applesauce gel you're trying out? It's hot!" He smiles. "Yes, you know you're a stud baby, don't you?" I carry him back into the living room just as Mike returns with my glass.

"Here ya go." He takes Kevin from me and I hand him the towel, which he stares at before he realizes. "Oh, duh," he mutters, drying off his son and returning to the news.

I pat my long, knotted hair with the second towel and head upstairs. "I need to borrow your clothes, Cess! I'm coming up!"

"In my room!"

I find her in a fresh pair of jeans and a yellow blouse,

her favorite color. "Thought you'd get all nice and comfy before helping a wounded girl out? Rude!"

She chuckles, "I was drenched!"

"So am I!" She smacks my arm as I pass her for the walk-in closet. "I'm going to borrow one of your pre-baby dresses."

She grumbles, "Someone's gotta wear them."

"You'll lose the weight."

"I highly doubt it."

Thumbing through the hangers I offer, "Well, you could cut out gluten."

"Don't even start, Meagan."

I hold up a very pretty, dark red, wrap number. "Will this look good on me?"

She cocks her eyebrows. "Don't make me punch you. I love that dress. Take it and be quiet."

As I peel off my wet clothes, dry off and slip on her neglected garment, I tell my big sister the facts. "If you change nothing, nothing changes. You know I went gluten-free because of my allergy to all the crap they're putting in our wheat in order to mass-produce food for the surplus population."

"Yes, yes, I know," she mumbles, interrupting me while sifting through the kit. "It forced you to find new things to eat. That got you into cooking. Then you wouldn't shut up about it and I was brilliant enough to say, 'Hey Meagan, why don't you go to culinary school and put your money where your mouth is?' and you, for once, took my advice. And now you're going to be an amazing chef I'll read about in magazines. I think this gauze is the right size, don't you?"

"Ooooooh, I like the sound of that famous in magazines part. Say it again."

"You can't eat bread."

Snatching a bobby pin from the pile on her dresser I throw it.

She ducks, laughing, "Sit down so I can fix you up."

Plopping onto her bed I watch my second mom gingerly peel away my soaked bandage. Since she was older and mom and dad both had to work, Cess helped raise me and Devin.

She blows on my stitches and then waves her hand, creating a breeze to dry them off while she reaches for the ointment. "Are you in pain?"

"It hurts like hell."

"They give you drugs?"

"Prescription, but you know me."

"No drugs."

"Not if I can help it. They shot me up before the stitches, and frankly my head was hurting so badly I could hardly see and didn't realize what they were doing until the needle was poked in my skin. So it's not as bad as…" My mind wanders back to Jeremy's where my head felt like someone had hit it with two hammers. I mutter to myself, "What a jerk that guy was."

"What guy?"

"The one I almost hit."

With goop on the pad of her ring finger, she pauses. "You mentioned him on the phone. Who was this guy?"

"Some asshole who thinks women can't drive."

Cecily smiles a little. "Wonder why he thinks that?"

"True."

She smiles, "Uh-huh. Think it's totaled?"

"Probably. Maybe? I'll find out soon." She tenderly applies the ointment while I continue, "Can't believe I left my phone in the car. I bet there are a million messages from Bryan, just beeping away in some junkyard. Ouch!"

"Shhh, I'm all done. There. Now let's dry your hair out." She pats it with the towel and starts to comb it like she did when I was a kid. It's a sweet feeling and I begin to relax, love warming me. I meet her eyes, but a sad smile appears on her face. I know what she's going to say even before her lips part. "Remember when Devin stopped letting me comb his hair?"

"He was five?"

"No, he was four," she sighs, blinking away the emotion. "Such a little man even then. He never liked me babying him." Straightening up she says, "Let me get my blow dryer. I'll put it on low near your forehead. Don't worry."

I know she disappeared to wipe her eyes, because that's what I'm doing. We try not to dwell on the loss. We try really damn hard. Grief is a sneaky thing, though. It plays a mean game of Hide and Seek.

Soon my hair is dry and Cecily smiles at me in her maternal way. "There. All better."

"Thanks, Cess."

"You're welcome, hon. Guess we have to Google your chef friend, since you don't know his number."

"Friend?"

"What is he then? Boss? Mentor?" she smiles, trying to pull the secret out of me. "Lover?"

"Better."

Her eyebrows twitch up. "What's better than that?"

"A man who holds the keys to your future dream. So don't anger him."

She laughs and walks to dig out the phone from her purse. "Oooo, I'm scared." Dropping the smile she dryly informs me, "I can handle Bryan Marchand. He has nothing I need."

8

JEREMY

Jogging up to the house I hear an unfamiliar cell phone ring and realize it's coming from *her* phone. Mine is off, that's for fucking sure. Just the way I like it.

Aslan waits for me to unlock the door, both of us panting and needing water. I ran us hard.

We run five times every day so I can stay ahead of my ghosts. Since we skipped the morning run due to the accident I really pushed us just now.

I'm living off the inheritance Grandpa Jerald left us all when he died, that and the money I made as a Marine. Spent little of what I earned while I was overseas. And you save a lot when you don't have to pay rent.

My brother Jaxson used his inheritance to buy his ranch property an hour north of Atlanta, just after college.

Justin used his to pay off Yale, where he'd gone away from his twin, Jason, for the first time so he could become the senator he is today.

Jason bought a sound studio and outfitted it with the best equipment, and saved a bunch. Now that he's married he told me the rest of what Grandpa left him is saved to put toward his kids' colleges. Since he's set on having at least four, it'll be stretched to breaking, but he and his wife do well for themselves.

Jake plans to buy Uncle Don out of his construction business someday and I know the huge house he and his wife live in now was paid for mostly by Grandpa.

What Jett did with his money I don't know. One day I might have to ask him, but I doubt I will.

I let mine simmer and compound in investments until after I left the Marines. I had no need for it then. My house is paid for. I live on little. I've lived on less so I don't need much.

But while my dog loves to get outside, Rottweilers aren't Labs or Greyhounds. They're not built for the kind of shit I put him through.

I need to get a handle on my life.

My family has hinted at all kinds of help I could get to clear my head of the guilt and traumatic stress. I haven't taken their advice because I don't believe in therapy. I'm a Marine. Not only that but I'm a Cocker, goddammit. We handle our own problems. It makes us stronger. I'll claw my way out of this darkness somehow, someday. And I'll stand tall when I do. Until then, I stand tall when I run. Getting physical gets me out of my head and into my body. My body I trust. My head is a dangerous neighborhood I don't like to go in alone. A friend told me that phrase. I can't claim it, but it's so fucking true.

I'm too late. The call has gone to Meagan's voicemail. But while I'm standing here staring at the screen a text comes through from the same person, someone named Cess.

Answer the phone, asshole. It's Meagan.

Snorting, I type, *No,* and hit send.

The phone rings in my hand.

I swipe to answer, "Pizza delivery."

"You told my boss I was in your bed? Are you crazy?"

With the sound of Aslan lapping water from his dish in the background I sit on the arm of my old couch. "I see you're feeling better. On drugs?"

"Do you have mental issues?"

Losing my amusement I explain, "I told him I was kidding. I have five brothers. We mess with each other. Get a sense of humor, Meagan Forrester."

"We aren't related! I don't even know you. And that was my life you were messing with!"

"Calm down, princess. He knows you still idolize him and only him. Your dysfunctional relationship is safe."

She's silent. When she speaks again her voice is quieter. "You're a serious jerk, you know that? Stop going through my phone."

"Don't worry. I got bored quick. Barely skimmed the surface before I found something more interesting to do with my time." I get up and head for the kitchen. Aslan looks up at me from his dish. His nub wags, slobber dripping from his sharp teeth as he pants a, *hey, Jeremy, where ya been?*

Meagan informs me in a voice you'd use for a child, "I need my phone. Listen to me very carefully. Put it down and do not touch it until I get there. Then you will hand it to me and we will never see each other again. Understand?"

Grabbing a used dishtowel I wipe Aslan's jaw and gums as I tell her, "No comprende. Could you say that a little slower? I only speak Spanish."

"Don't. Touch. Telefono." She hangs up.

I chuckle all the way into my bathroom, grabbing the half-used toothpaste and searching my cabinet for whatever else I can use for this funny joke I just thought up. A back-up bottle of shampoo, a bar of soap and then I'm heading into my bedroom, scanning.

"You'll do," I mutter, adding a worn paperback copy of Game of Thrones to my collection of oddities.

"Wait, didn't Mom give me some coasters?" Searching my closet I find the box. They have pictures of Atlanta neighborhood signs, so I choose West Midtown, because it's where I live.

Carrying my crazy stash into the living room I shove it all into her purse.

"That's pretty good. But I need something else. What else? She's into food, huh? I think Mom gave me a cake mix, didn't she?"

I run to search for it and find it collecting dust. Snatching it off the shelf I laugh all the way back into the living room where I suddenly stop walking.

When was the last time I laughed?

9

MEAGAN

Since Mike had to go to work and it's time for Kevin's nap, I ignored Cecily's commands that I stay at her place and rest, and instead called for a Lyft driver to take me to the jerk's house.

I only use Lyft, because I found out that in order to be approved as a driver you must get interviewed, someone from the company comes and checks out your vehicle, and they do background checks on you.

Frankly that last one is reason enough for me to choose them, since I'm a woman. You never know who's on the other side of a computer filling out an online form to drive us around. Alone.

When it comes to putting my life in the hands of strangers, call me crazy but I like to be smart and I like to be safe.

"Just wait here, please. I have to run in and grab

something and then my next stop is Buckhead where my boss lives."

The Lyft driver reaches down and produces an umbrella. "Use this."

"Awww, thank you!" Snapping it open outside the door, I step out in the knee-high black boots and short trench coat I borrowed from Cecily, hastily making my way up the path to Jeremy's house. It's just a skeleton of a yard. No attention has been paid to it save for mowing the grass. There are dirt patches where bushes should be. No flowers anywhere. What a pit.

A deep and low bark comes from within as I close the umbrella and knock. The door swings open and Jeremy leans on the doorframe in a pair of jeans and a white tank top, his hair freshly shampooed. He scans my new outfit from wet boots to dry head, and smirks as he meets my eyes. "Gave yourself an upgrade."

Why do I have to be attracted to jerks?

"Where's my phone? Did you by any chance get my purse, too? A car is waiting to take me to work."

"Your god sent a limo so he could whisk you to his mountain?"

"Yes. He's out there waiting for me right now."

Jeremy starts to lean out so he can see. I push on his stone-like chest to stop him. "Don't be so nosy!"

He glances to my fingers and smirks with mockery, "Now Meagan, not polite to enter a man's personal space when you're being rude to him. You're touching my chest."

"So go get my purse and I'll be on my way."

Jeremy gazes at me, mischief in his eyes. To avoid him running out and trying to meet Bryan in the flesh, who is of course not here, I shove the umbrella into Jeremy and push us both into his home as I explode, "Fine! I'll get it myself. Hold this!" I shut us both safely inside and glance to his dog. "Is he dangerous?"

"Only when I want him to be."

The dog and I eye each other. "Which is not right now, yes?"

"You're safe. But don't move too fast," Jeremy warns me.

"I can see the smile in your eyes, but I'm not taking any chances, so... *nice doggie*." I carefully pick up my purse. "Is the phone in here?"

"Yes."

"I can tell I'm tired. This feels really heavy. My umbrella, please?"

He doesn't give it to me, so I cock an eyebrow. "Stop treating me like a sister."

"I don't have any sisters."

"Well, if you had one, this is how you'd treat her. I

should know. So stop it. We're not related and we're not friends."

"We could be."

This statement throws me a little. I take a deep breath and give a quick glance around the nearly empty house. "That's not possible for reasons I'm too nice to tell you. Now give me my umbrella, please. It belongs to *my* sister or I'd just leave without it."

Can't really tell him it's the Lyft driver's, now can I?

"This umbrella?" He holds it high over his head.

"I am hoping you will be a gentleman and cut the nonsense."

Frowning he hands it over. "I was just having fun."

"Well, I wasn't."

"Goodbye Meagan."

"Goodbye weirdo."

He chuckles and pets his dog's head, both of them facing me like they're my goodbye-committee. With my hand on the doorknob, I pause and glance at him from under my eyelashes to admit, "Well, okay, I was having a little fun."

Suppressing a smile I stroll out the door, pop the umbrella open and hurry into the rain.

The driver is not in the line of sight from here, thank God.

I know Jeremy is watching me.

I can feel it.

Confirming my suspicion I hear his deep voice call out from behind me, "We might become friends, Meagan Forrester, age twenty-five, penchant for oral hygiene!"

Snorting with laughter I call back, "No, we won't be! I'm not friends with people who snoop through my stuff!"

I glance over my shoulder, and pause. He's standing in the downpour, his short dark hair matted to his angular face. The white tank top is transparent now that it's soaked, plastered to his muscles, his taut nipples straining against it. The jeans are getting wetter by the second.

So am I.

He tips his head, but makes no move to go inside where it's nice and dry.

Confused, I turn around, blood pumping harder as I hurry to the car. He obviously doesn't have a penny to his name. I wouldn't be surprised if he burgled houses to pay the rent. He's way too devilish to hold a real job or have a boss. None of these are qualities I'm looking for in a man, so why is it so hard to keep walking? I desperately want to turn back around and undress him.

Climbing into the Lyft I decide it's just chemistry, and that's something you can't control. Choices, you can. I will forget about him. I just need to get away from here as quickly as possible because I've begun to throb.

"Can you back up and go the other way?"

The driver asks, "Wait, what?"

"Don't drive straight. I don't want to pass in front of his door. You see, my boyfriend and I just broke up and he's crying out there. It's embarrassing. For him. For me. For you. Just back up and I'll tip you extra."

"Whatever you say."

"Thank you." Opening up my purse I dig around and frown at a cement coaster that's not mine, but it's of West Midtown, where I live. Did Bryan give me this and I didn't notice?

Wait, what the fuck is Game of Thrones doing here? Did I put this in my bag before I left? I read this novel years ago. And what the hell is this yellow cake mix? And this half-used toothpaste that's not my brand, and this soap and shampoo?

"Oh my God," I mutter, smiling despite myself. "Jeremy, you're such a weirdo!"

The driver meets my eyes in the rearview. "Your ex make you laugh?"

"Yes. He's very strange."

"Think you might get back together?"

Staring out at the rain, I mutter, still smiling at the joke he played. "Nope. I'll never see him again."

10

JEREMY

"What time is it?" I ask Aslan with my face squished in the pillow. Meant to take a short nap since I had nothing better to do, but now I feel like shit after the damn nightmare.

Lifting my head I scan the nearby vicinity for my phone, but of course it's not here. It's shoved into my dresser, or a jacket I wore, or some jeans lying in a pile somewhere. And I don't have a clock in my room so I have no clue how late it is.

It wasn't easy to kick the habit of waking up before dawn. This was my time now, not theirs, but I was so trained it was hard to believe I didn't have to jump to attention for anyone. I could do whatever the fuck I wanted and top of the list was sleep.

Didn't know the nightmares would make that goal an empty one.

It's dark out, but that doesn't mean much.

It's February. Sun sets early.

Rolling onto my back I pet my buddy who must have climbed onto the bed when I was out. Maybe I thrashed about and he came to soothe me. Aslan's good at that. Happy I'm awake, he rests his heavy chin on my chest and stares at me, in no hurry to rise. I took him running three times today so far. He was probably hoping my eyes would stay shut for the rest of the night.

"You're off the hook pal. I've got somewhere I want to be for once."

He lifts his head.

"Go ahead and stay here. Rest." I drop my legs over the side of the bed and stand up, stretching before I begin the search for my phone. "Have I spoken to anyone since the car wreck three days ago? Oh right, Jake."

Opening the door I glance outside and see it resting on a windowpane right where anyone could have seen it and stolen it. The battery's gone dead. "Nice," I mutter, heading inside to plug in the cord and talk to Jake while tethered to an outlet.

"I thought maybe you changed your mind," he answers, not so subtly hiding how relieved he is I didn't disappear.

"Nah. You home?"

"Sure am."

"I'm on my way in ten. Gotta wash off."

"Please do. I don't want you stinking up my best suit."

"Then maybe I'll skip bathing."

He chuckles and mutters, "I'll see you soon."

The shower is hotter than hell on the devil's birthday. After so many cold, recycled ones in foreign, desolate places, I don't feel clean unless I fry the skin right off my bones.

But tonight something's new. My dick is hard for the first time in too long, so I give it a few strokes and urge it to come to life. Feels good. Doesn't take a rocket scientist to tell me I'm attracted to that girl Meagan. Her beautiful brown eyes are the first image that pops into my head as I stroke my cock. Takes no time at all for the surge of hunger to rise from my core. I'm rock hard and aroused to the point that I'm gritting my teeth before drowning my head in the stream, blistering heat cascading down my face, chest, abs and everywhere below.

Those boots she was wearing.

Oh man, I love a woman in boots.

Even better if that's the only thing she's wearing. Just her, naked in those, asking me, *You know who's a god, Jeremy? You are.*

Oh fuck, yes.

What man doesn't want to hear that?

We'd bend over backwards to make a woman happy if she looked at us like we're her hero. I know she's got her mind set on that asshole, Bryan, but is her heart set on him?

We'll see.

I stiffen as my erection expands and pulses my juice into the hot stream. Standing here, reveling in the aftershocks, I palm my cock for a good minute, to enjoy the buzz.

When Jake answers his front door of the beautiful two-story he and Drew moved into, he predictably tells me to take off my shoes. Some things never change.

I kick them off and he hugs me.

I cough and step back, shoving my hands in my jeans pockets. My family, they're so worried about me. Jake and I were best friends growing up, the two youngest *and* we're the only ones who got Mom's coloring so we look a lot alike, too. But we haven't quite gotten back to that old friendship we once had. There's a distance now. He's cautious of me, doesn't want to scare me off. I just want him to stop treating me like I'm traumatized. Even though in many ways I am.

"Where's my pretty sister-in-law?"

"Out back with Emma and her new pet turtle. Ethan and the new baby are with them, too. You want to go say hello?"

"Can I do it another time? I'm in a hurry."

He nods and we walk to his room in silence. "How're you doin' Jeremy?"

"Hangin' in there."

Jake glances to me. "You didn't tell me what you need my suit for."

"I know."

A rueful smile flashes on him and we go inside. He heads for the closet and I glance around, a little in awe of how dramatically his life changed since we were roommates. I pictured Jake as the last of us to settle down, he was such a player. Justin I *never* thought would, jaded bastard that he was. And yet they're both married now. All five of my brothers are happily hitched. It's nutty.

I'm the last one, and I can't imagine going down that path. What do I have to give anyone? I shut my heart down in the Marines. I had to. Everyone has to, even though you believe that one day you'll be able to be normal again. I thought that once. But then I lost a friend out there who took the last open pieces with him.

Jake walks out carrying a black suit on a wooden hanger. "So you're not going to tell me what this is for?"

"Nah."

I see his energy change.

Time to brace myself.

"Jeremy —"

"—Don't, Jake. Just let it be."

I can see his frustration. It's extreme as he gets in my face. "Why're you shutting me out?"

"I'm not," I shrug.

"Yeah, you fuckin' are."

"I'm in a hurry. I'm not meaning to shut you out, Jake!"

"Bullshit!"

Losing my cool I jab a finger into his chest. "You have to stop treating me like I'm fragile! Asking how I am all the time. It doesn't help. It only reminds me that I'm different than I was. And I don't want to go back to who I used to be. I'm proud I served. I'm proud I changed. I just need to find out who I am now that I'm a fuckin' civilian again, Jake! Give me time. Get off my back!"

We're about to come to blows. His eyes darken and he takes a step backwards. "Fine," he mutters.

"Fine," I parrot.

"If you're going to borrow this suit you have to tell me why, or no deal."

On an exhale I cross my arms. "Jesus, really?"

"Yes, fuckin' really! I know you need time, Jeremy, but I miss my best friend. You're leaving me out of this, everything you're going through! I know I wasn't there. I wasn't in your platoon, I can never know what it was like. But

I'm your family, man. I love you. And you're fuckin' killing me here. Stop shutting me out! Tell me why you need the suit?"

Gritting my teeth I ask him, no, I'm almost begging him, "Let me tell you when I return it."

"No! Now!"

"Come on!" I throw my fingers in my hair and pace around holding my head. "Just give me the damn suit."

"Why when you return it? How come you want to wait 'til then to tell me? I don't get it. Help me understand!"

Rubbing my face, I think about my options. There are none if I want this, and I don't know why but I do want it.

I need that suit.

I'm not leaving without it, which means I have to confess that I'm a little fuckin' nervous. Which isn't like me, and it sure the hell ain't like him.

We Cocker Brothers don't get nervous.

I let out a roar and shout, "BECAUSE WHAT IF IT DOESN'T GO WELL!? Huh?!"

He stares at me, blinking like he's catching on. "Wait, does this have to do with a girl?"

I meet his eyes but say nothing.

Jake's open mouth spreads into a grin. "Holy shit! You found someone you like?"

"Not long term. She's just fun to mess with. That's it!"

He strides quickly to me and claps my left shoulder like this is the best news he's heard since I got back in one piece and surprised him at that family BBQ when Emma was just over a year old and Ethan was on the way. And Sofia. And Ben.

"Holy shit, Jeremy! Take the suit. You need some shoes?"

A lopsided smile twists my mouth and I shrug, "Yeah, I guess I could use some."

He glances to my combat boots, chuckles and heads into the closet. "You didn't even think about it did you?" Two seconds later he appears and tosses a pair of shiny black dress shoes at me. "These are my best. If you scuff 'em, I don't care! Have fun for fuck's sake. Please for the love of God have some fun."

"Can I change here? I'm in a hurry and you just made me more late."

He laughs and uses his middle finger to flip me off, then twists his wrist and points that 'fuck you' to the bathroom. Soon I'm walking out in a white button-up and snug suit that fits so well I look like I'm some sort of playboy. "I look good in this."

He smirks, "So do I. Bring it back."

"Can you tie this for me?"

He wraps the slender black necktie around my collar,

meets my eyes and mutters, "Grandpa Jerald taught me how to do this."

"Yeah? He never taught me."

"Guess he thought I'd teach it to you. I never got around to it."

"Never had the need."

Jake comfortably tightens it, pats my chest, and says, "There." He backs up and inspects me. "Go look at yourself."

I smirk, cocking one eyebrow. "I know I make this look good."

Jake grins and shakes his head. "Jesus, it's good to see you again."

"You saw me last Friday at Mom and Dad's."

"That wasn't you. This light in your eyes? This is my brother."

11

MEAGAN

One of Le Marchand's biggest investors points at my head. "What happened to you?"

My hair has a deep side-part to cover the bandage, but she's the type of woman who looks for flaws in everything. Especially other women.

"I was mugged," I lie.

Her hand flutters to her broach on a gown that's a tad overdone. "Oh my! Where? Not near the restaurant?!"

Oh shit.

Amusing plan backfiring.

Retreat! Retreat!

"No, of course not. Your investment is safe. You know that. Buckhead is the best neighborhood in Atlanta. This happened downtown, near a really dark Marta stop."

"Oh, what a relief," she sighs before sipping from her elegant champagne flute. "What were you doing down there?

I never leave Buckhead."

Of course you don't.

"You know those clowns that are going around?"

"Clowns?" she repeats, unable to frown from all the injections.

"The men dressed up as clowns who go around robbing people? It's all over the news."

"I hadn't heard! How horrifying!"

I lean in and hush my voice dramatically, "And not just in one city, either. Across the country! People are picking up the trend and they don't even know each other. It's terrible, isn't it? So scary!"

As she stares at me in horror, Bryan, basking in the limelight of his pre-grand opening party, strolls up to us in a five-thousand-dollar suit. His mid-length wavy hair is styled and his smile is pure star-material. My heart jumps as he winks at me and then touches her back. "Eleanor! So glad you could make it. This gown is stunning. Too bad you're married. Did I hear I missed out on cooking for your thirty-fifth birthday celebration because we hadn't opened yet?"

Her face transforms into frozen joy upon sight of him. "Oh Bryan, add thirty years and you're close to the right number! Dear man, what a success! I haven't tasted your infamous cuisine yet but this champagne is to die for. I was just talking to your assistant about the strangest thing."

"His apprentice," I correct her. "I'm a chef, too."

She glances to me.

Bryan interjects, "Eleanor, we have an emergency in the kitchen and I need Meagan. Mind if I borrow her from you?"

I give the investor my most gracious smile. "It was an absolute pleasure speaking with you. You do look lovely. Please excuse me. I was so enjoying our chat."

"Of course, dear. I'm so sorry about your—"

"—Oh, thank you!" I cut her off so Bryan doesn't hear the lie I just told about being mugged by vigilante clowns. Turning to him, I brightly ask, "Ready?"

His blue eyes gleam and we stroll off. Not touching, of course. He never touches me in public. After a safe distance he whispers to me, "You're doing very well with the guests. I'm impressed."

"Thank you," I smile.

If only he knew.

Invites for this party were extended only to donors, trade magazines, local periodicals, and huge profile names in the city.

Because Bryan is a famous chef, he's even attracted journalists from the huge magazines I subscribe to, Bon Appétit and Gourmet. This being the first restaurant with his name on it and where he isn't creating his delicacies for someone else's acclaim, it is crucial to Le Marchand's success that tonight impresses one and all.

So far so good.

"Did you want me to help the sous chef?" I ask, hopeful that's why he came to get me.

"Are you kidding?" he mutters out of the corner of his mouth while waving to a wealthy male investor saluting him with a glass of cognac. "You're not ready for that. I need you to keep an eye on the hostess. She's getting drunk and doesn't think I noticed her flirting with the wealthy men in order to skim cocktails off them."

My spirits drop.

"But I thought you said I was needed in the kitchen?"

"Well, you had just called yourself a chef in front of Eleanor Riggins so I had to make it believable. I couldn't exactly say our hostess is sipping bourbon, could I?"

"But I am a chef!"

"Go take care of it." Bryan leaves my side to charm a table of four of the best dressed at the party, leaving me no choice but to do what he says and quit arguing.

Walking toward the front door I lock onto Mira, the stunning blonde he hired because *the first person a guest sees in my establishment should be ravishing*, his words.

Her smile does light up the foyer.

I think the potted plants we paid a fortune for may

have bloomed in the last hour under her shining light, she's that pretty.

Which means I am not excited to have her around. I have not secured Bryan as mine, yet, and with a girl like her representing the face of Le Marchand it could be weeks, days, minutes, before he's texting her to come over at two o'clock in the morning, and not me.

Even if I'm not a fan I can't have her drunk tonight. I care about the success of this restaurant almost as much as he does. It's my chance to make a name for myself. How often do people my age get to be affiliated with such a powerful reputation as Bryan's when they're just starting out?

Inhale patience, Meagan.

Go do what is not in your job description. Go tell Blonde Perfection to cut it out so her smile can last the night.

Bryan doesn't need a drunk and passed-out greeter. Every article, online and otherwise, would lead with this story: Le Marchand's bar was a bigger hit than his kitchen.

Wait…what the hell is *he* doing here?

My eyes zip up and down, drinking in Jeremy Cocker. His suit fits him like his lover is the tailor. The smile he gives Mira is more dazzling than hers.

She completely loses her cool, eyelashes fluttering as her back hunches over on a gushing smile. "Welcome to Le Marchand. May I have your exclusive invitation?"

With a throaty gravel he casually tells her, like he's James Fucking Bond, "I left it on the passenger seat of my new Audi A8. Shall I have the valet retrieve it for me?"

I did not know that you could make shaking your head flirty, but she manages, saying with a giggle, "That won't be necessary! We'll overlook it just this once."

"Just this once?" he asks, with a cocked eyebrow so sexy I want to slap it off of him.

Standing just a few feet away from them, I throw my hands on my hips and stare.

She leans in a little to whisper, "Well, maybe more than once."

"Mira!" I didn't mean to bark that so loudly.

They both look over at me, and his eyes alight with amusement. Wait, he doesn't look surprised that I'm standing here.

He found out about this event!

He's come here to mess with my head.

What an asshole! My eyes steel as I begin to announce he doesn't have an invite. I know he doesn't because I'm the one who sent them out! And I'd bet these Jimmy Choo shoes that he doesn't have a fucking Audi, either.

I open my mouth…

"What the fuck're you doin' here?" Senator Justin Cocker strolls up to the three of us, dressed to impress, eyes sparkling as he touches my shoulder. "Meagan, I see you've met my brother Jeremy. He's single by the way. The last of us to fall."

My mouth clamps shut as the two men hug. Oh my God. No way. No, no, way.

The Cocker Brothers, the EMT said. *Six of the most*...but how could I have seen this coming?

Everyone knows who Justin Cocker is. His rise to Senate was explosively unique. Him I did send an invitation to and was proud to announce to Bryan that he'd accepted, when I'd gotten the R.S.V.P.

But I never had a clue these two were related, despite the name, for obvious reasons if you saw them standing face-to-face as they are right now. Justin is a towheaded blonde with pale green eyes, six foot three, svelte in looks and demeanor, the perfect politician. Jeremy's coloring is the opposite, dark and brooding. He's stocky. Lives in a shack. And acts like a fucking child.

Is he adopted?

The only thing they have in common is the amused glints in their eyes. As they talk, and Mira and I watch from very different, interested points of view, the two men rib each other how only brothers can, their smirks equally hot, equally mind-boggling.

"Well, shit if I knew you were gonna be here I

would've gone to a hot dog stand and skipped it," Jeremy says.

Justin volleys back, "Hot dogs? Is that what they're calling it? So…you've finally gone gay?"

"Nah, you already had that covered. I like to be unique."

"Which is why you're wearing—"

Jeremy cuts him off, "A suit like I wear every other night I avoid you like the plague?"

Justin laughs, his famous white teeth flashing. He slides his hands in his pockets and jogs his chin to the party. "Politics. I'm trying to get the Governor on my side about term-limit reform. He has friends in the Democratic Party. He's a Republican, but he's that good he appeals to both sides to get things done. Otherwise we're in a standstill. Guess you could say I'm learning from him."

And I'm learning that I need to get better at making myself scarce when I'm in shock. I'm standing here parked on the gorgeous rug I talked Bryan into buying, gawking, albeit with my mouth clamped shut.

Mira isn't any better than I am.

She's staring, too.

Only she's doing it from behind longer eyelashes.

Jeremy glances to me like he just remembered I'm here. "You were saying?"

The bastard knows I was about to give him the boot, and now I can't. "Mira! Show this man to a table! Don't you know he's Justin Cocker's brother?"

Jeremy's eyes glitter, and Justin side-eyeballs me with an emotionless 'I couldn't care less about you' expression.

I exit with very little composure, even though I think I'm strolling away with the appearance of authority. Were I to be watching myself from above I would see that I look pretty damn lame.

12

JEREMY

Highlighted in a sexy-as-hell, tight, white, ladies-cut pantsuit, Meagan's ass swings with indignation as she disappears into the crowd. I glance ahead of her direction and see the bar four deep with people clamoring for a drink. She's probably headed there to inspect something.

I think she's a manager. That's how she acted. Pretty young to be one, but okay. I'm interested.

I didn't expect to see Justin here, though of course he would be. He travels in these circles to maintain his social and political connections in order to get things done. My brother has turned out to be an impressive man, far more than he showed when he was younger. I used to think he was a dick. Now I look up to him after how he handled that crazy fucking election. Amazing.

"Come with me," he smiles. "I want to introduce you to the Governor."

"Great," I nod, thinking to myself that I couldn't have planned how well that just went. Meagan was about to throw me out on my ass. To watch her eat her unspoken words was fucking hilarious.

As we make our way through the crowded restaurant, Justin asks, "Jake's suit, huh? I recognize it because he's got only one."

"He loaned it to me, and you were about to call me out back there."

Justin chuckles, "But you caught it just in time."

"Trying to make me look bad in front of the ladies," I smirk. He laughs and doesn't deny it. "Fucker. Hey, can I meet you at the table? I want to get a drink at the bar, have a look around."

"Sure. We're right over there." He motions to a booth where three conservatively dressed Republicans, two men and one woman, sit deep in conversation.

"You need anything, Justin?"

"I'm covered. Waitress has been paying us extra attention."

"Lucky you."

He laughs and heads off.

There are five exits—that's the first thing I take note of. Second are the ten chandeliers. If a bomb hit this place, glass would be shrapnel.

As I casually cross the room, I develop a strategy for how I'd evacuate the civilians. Even if I'm one of them now, if shit went down they could count on me to get them safely out of here. If the enemy came in from the front, I'd...

Stop it, Jeremy. Get your blood pressure back to normal. You're in Buckhead, where you grew up. Upper class Atlanta, Georgia, and there are no terrorists stalking the perimeters. Everyone just wants to eat a good meal and act like they're okay.

Start pretending you believe the lie, too.

As I walk up to the bar I sidestep the line to where I can hear her talking to one of the bartenders, a good-looking older man who keeps working as he leans to hear what she has to say from over the counter.

"If Mira comes asking for a shot ignore her."

"Shit, Meagan, she already had one. She said you wouldn't mind."

She contains it pretty well, but I can tell she wants to fire the hostess five minutes ago. I caught the name *Mira* when she practically shouted it back there, and her fuse was short.

Meagan lowers her voice and I have to lean in to hear her tell him, "No one should be drinking when they're on the clock. Not you. Not her. No one. Are we together on this now?"

"Yes of course. Sorry." It's clear he respects her, which

impresses me. He's gotta be at least ten years her senior. She must have done something to earn him deferring to her so quickly and without a glint of hesitation or ego in his eyes.

The line is moving and I'm not in it, so it appears like I'm waiting to talk to her.

Which I am. Not cool.

Stepping to my left I cut in front of a woman and her elegant friend, both early forties, dressed to impress. They pause their conversation, looking at me like they can't believe I just walked right in like I'd been here the whole time. "You two look gorgeous this evening. Your husbands didn't step up to get your cocktails for you? What are they, crazy?" Both pairs of eyes slide down my body as they size me up.

The brunette says, "Look at you, so smooth."

"Think you can play us?" the sandy-brown haired one asks.

I give them my best smirk and lean in, holding their looks, one at a time as I speak. "Am I that transparent? Must have lost my talent somewhere along the way."

The brunette fingers her necklace. "I doubt that."

The line moves up and it's my turn. "What are you ladies having? Wait, let me guess." To the brunette I narrow my eyes, trying to pinpoint her flavor. "Gin martini. Dirty." She brightens with surprise.

I nailed it.

Flicking my chin I gaze at the sandy-brown haired woman. "Tequila. Neat." She practically snorts, and I give her a big smile. I knew that was the wrong guess. "I'm kidding. You're not going to drink a tequila shot at an event such as this. But I bet you do when you're alone." She blushes, shocked, turning to her friend like *that is not true,* when it clearly is. "Here you'd drink a thick red, like a Malbec or Red Zinfandel." Her eyebrows dance upward with a gleam in her eyes.

"How did you do that?"

"I was a bartender before I joined the Marines." I turn away from where this topic is headed because I'm trying not to think about my service tonight, and I don't want these women asking me a bunch of questions about my time in. Ordering our drinks from the bartender Meagan was talking to I glance around and realize she left, and I can't see her anywhere in the dining room.

Well, that didn't go as planned.

After telling him what the ladies will be having, I order a Sweetwater Imperial Stout in the bottle so I can get out of here. I drop some cash down, covering the cost of their drinks, too, grab my beer and tip my head. "Ladies. It's been a pleasure."

"Do you have to go?" the brunette asks, despite her wedding ring.

"My brother is waiting for me. Nice meeting you both. Enjoy your evening."

Strolling away I scan the room again for Meagan. I don't want to sit at a stuffy table listening to political debates. No serious conversations tonight. I want to entertain myself and I'm intent on doing just that. With a quiet desperation.

Something crashes and my eyes cut right. A young male bartender is trying to keep up with the number of guests craving booze. There are three working back there, but it's not enough with that inexperienced kid in the lineup.

I watch him from a distance as his nerves become more frazzled. An irate woman starts barking at him. I'm too far away to hear, but I can tell she's pissed her drink is taking forever after she's waited this long. Compelled to watch, I make my way through the crowd, eyes on him. The kid is on the verge of tears. Really jittery as he pours ice into a fresh shaker. The party guest reaches over with a gesture of STOP and he blinks up at her. I push my way through the lines and overhear her bark, "That's the one you dropped! You haven't cleaned it!"

He's frozen now. Out of ideas. In over his head.

Completely unplanned I walk around the bar and offer a confident smirk to the guest, "Hey gorgeous, God, I'm sorry you had to wait so long but we'll take care of that drink right now and it's on the house. What did you order?" I take the shaker from the kid and glance around for a new one. There's no back up so I step over to the sink and give her my best smile while I clean it.

"Belvedere martini!"

The kid steps back with his mouth open, not recognizing me and wondering why a guy in a suit has taken over. He probably thinks I'm an investor. There's no way he'll try and stop me from bailing him out.

"Comin' right up," I wink while drying off the shaker before I spring into action like I'm twenty-one-years-old again working in those nightclubs with a lot more people than this clamoring to get drunk.

I scoop ice into the cleaned shaker, plus into an empty martini glass to chill it. Splash Vermouth into the shaker, toss it around, then pour it out through the strainer so that it only coats the ice. More than that and it's too strong. You don't want to overpower the main act especially with a high-end vodka like Belvedere. I flip the slender, elegantly engraved vodka bottle in the air, catch it upside down and pour over the flavored ice.

With one hand I hammer the silver shaker in the air until the vodka crystalizes. Toss the extra ice out of the glass and now that it's chilled and foggy. I flip the shaker over, high in the air above the rim and strain the martini into it, the cascading stream so long it looks like I might miss.

But I don't.

It's all about the presentation.

The once unhappy guest is now watching like I'm a miracle worker, and when I hand her the martini, she beams at me, "Now that's a bartender!"

Three stylishly suited men step up to take her place. They've been watching and they're curious if I can be as good the second time. While I lean in to hear their order I catch the eyes of another man standing off to the side, not with this group, and not in line either. He's got mid-length wavy hair and blue eyes. He looks like he owns the place. In fact, it occurs to me he probably does. I'm staring at Bryan Marchand himself, and he's staring back.

He strolls up to the bar with his arms crossed as the three men see him and pause. They must know who he is because they're dying to know what he's about to say.

In a normal volume, more curious than anything, he says to me, "You don't work here."

"Nope."

"Keep going. Show me."

My ego cocks. We men are competitive to the point of being stupid. I speed up the entertaining presentation I'm capable of and make a Woodford Reserve Old Fashioned, a Ron Zacapa Rum Mojito, and a Don Julio Margarita—three very different cocktails, and the first two require muddling where you squash up a cherry and fresh mint, respectively. That shit takes time, and I'm on fire with the need to show him I can do it.

Despite the fact that I am not familiar with this particular bar and have to find the bottles necessary for the ingredients, I fly around without breaking a sweat, moving as smoothly as if I were seducing every person watching. I've gathered an audience. I can feel the eyes soaking in my every move and I have to admit, it's exciting. As I flip even the awkwardly square bottle of Woodford in the air it makes more faces shift in my direction.

In no time flat I land three perfect cocktails in front of the men. "Gentlemen."

The nervous-wreck kid is gone. Probably went to shit his pants in private.

They lift the glasses while I grab a towel and pretend to dry my hands, just for something to do while I wait for the verdict.

The first guy licks his lips. "Now that's an Old Fashioned."

The others nod and murmur similar remarks.

Approval all around and my smirk deepens as some people clap and say, "I want him making my drink!"

I feel good.

Free.

For the first time in years.

I'm trying to keep my cool and act like none of this matters. I lock eyes with Marchand and ask him, "What can I get you?"

Magnanimously he smiles and says to the crowd, and to me, "You want a job?"

Blinking away from him I fold the towel and place it on a clean surface, considering the offer. Meeting his eyes, I pause and say, "Count me in."

"I'm Bryan Marchand. This is my restaurant."

"Nice place."

We shake hands. If he only knew it was me on the phone that day.

"How much do we owe you?" the man with the Woodford Old Fashioned asks.

Marchand waves him off, "This one's on me, Kenny. Just make sure the write-up is a good one."

Kenny laughs and walks off with his buddies.

"That was the food critic for Bon Appétit you just impressed."

I keep my face cool. "Lucky him."

Marchand's smirk widens into a grin. "Lucky him," he chuckles, eyeing me. "You're a guest tonight. Join your friends. Give your number to my apprentice so we can put you on the schedule." Grabbing a passing busser he asks in a quiet voice, "Where the fuck is Ty?"

"Bathroom."

"Get him back here now." Bryan heads off to schmooze.

I pop a couple bottles of beer for the next guest and Ty pops back in looking terrified of losing his job.

"You okay, kid?"

"I got it," he mutters, irritated.

"Take it from here," I hand one of the guests a bottle of Orpheus. "Can you ring that up?"

"Oh, you can't do *everything*?"

I get in his face, my voice low. "Listen twerp, lose the attitude until you deserve to have one."

He swallows hard and backs up to let me out.

"Who's Marchand's right hand man?"

"Why?"

"Answer the question."

He mutters with a meek look, "Meagan Forrester,"

"No shit?" Off I go with a spring in my step. She wasn't around when I was back here. I looked. She's going to hate me working here and I can't wait to see her face. Passing Justin's table I slide in next to him.

"Where you been?" he asks, glancing at my empty hands. "Where's your drink?"

The other three politicians are heavy in an argument

about who the fuck cares. I lean over to whisper to my brother, "I just got a job."

His head swings back in a surprise. "As a hustler?"

I mutter through stifled laughter, "No, you fuck. Bartending."

"Oh, shit. That's right! I forgot you used to be one."

"Yep."

"You gonna be happy doin' it?"

"It cleared my head."

His sharp, green eyes flicker with relief. "Good. Then do it."

"Mind if I excuse myself? I have to give my number to the boss lady."

"Get it done. You coming back?"

I glance to the irate Republicans and lock eyes with Justin. "Probably not."

He chuckles through his nose, as my brother, not as a big mucky muck. "I fucking love your honesty, Jeremy."

"Learned it from you." I clap a hand on his shoulder and slide out of the booth. Before I take off, I point at him. "Don't shoot this one into the grape vine just yet. Don't know how long it'll last."

He mutters with disdain, "I'm not the one who calls everybody. Drives me fuckin' crazy. And Jeremy? It's good to see you smiling."

I shake my head at him, suppressing a grin because yeah, both brothers I saw today told me the exact same thing. And yes, I have to admit it feels good to hear it, and good to be around them.

Maybe I'll start spending more time with the family. But I don't think so yet. I'm just not ready for that kind of closeness. I need room to breathe. Being the youngest wasn't easy. Had to find my own voice as a man. Guess I'm still finding it. But all that love? Some people want it. For an introvert like me, it can be stifling.

I head off in search of my new lady boss.

A female in control of me.

Never had that before.

Should be fun.

13

MEAGAN

"Who're you?" The man straightens up from whispering in Mira's ear while she sips his bourbon. He glares at me despite his shining gold wedding band. Fucking skeezeball.

"I'm her boss, and I'm terribly sorry to have to interrupt, but I really need to talk to Mira about—" I almost say, *her disease,* but realize in time that would reflect badly on the restaurant. "—her promotion."

"Really?" my inebriated hostess brightly says. "Already?"

I prompt his exit again. "Would you mind? Work business."

He takes his elbow off the host stand and tells her a very slimy, "Congratulations."

When she doesn't respond or even look his way again, he awkwardly walks off.

Mira grabs my arm with a mild slur. "Promoted to server? They make so much more money."

Classy, Mira, classy.

"I was thinking bartender."

She's not sure if I'm serious. Beautiful dumbass.

"But I don't know how to make cocktails."

"You sure know how to drink them."

Her eyes go dead. "Oh. You're not promoting me, are you…"

"Do we have a problem here?"

"No," she whispers, embarrassed.

"We better not. Watch yourself. Drink some water. Coffee. Anything without alcohol content that will clear your head until your shift is up. That includes near beer. You're on the clock. On Bryan's dime. No more, you hear me?" I flip around and run right into the wall of muscle named Jeremy Cocker. "Oof!"

"Careful Boss Lady."

My eyelashes rise and I lock eyes with him. His sexy smirk triggers instant confusion, not to mention what he called me. I guess he overheard me reprimanding our hostess and now he knows I have some authority here. To pass him I step to the right, and he steps to the left, blocking me.

"Move!"

He chuckles and steps out of my way, and I quickly

return to the insanity of our pre-grand opening.

Entrée plates have been cleared from tables boasting beautiful floral centerpieces. Elegant desert dishes have taken their place, but even they have been scraped clean. Guests are smiling and happy and life is going pretty damn well. Outside of Mira's boozing and one cook fucking up three garnishes before I caught him, it's a much smoother night than Bryan or I anticipated.

But then Jeremy's deep voice ripples into my backside, "So, when do you want me back?"

I flip around and ask him in a volume only heard by us. "Have you been following me this whole time?"

He matches my quiet by leaning in, his voice husky. "You mean for a whole two minutes? Yes."

"Why?!"

"I need to know when you want me back."

His question makes no sense. "I never had you!" I blurt, totally impatient.

"Well you have me now."

We stare at each other and he's got that look in his eyes again, like he's on the verge of grinning. Some sort of private joke at my expense. Through gritted teeth I demand, "What are you talking about? I don't want you."

His eyes flicker like that stilled him. Or shocked him. But the smirk flashes back into place right before he says,

"It's not your decision to make."

"Come here!" I storm off to a server station where we're out of earshot of the guests. And of Bryan. If Jeremy Cocker is coming onto me he's picked the worst time to do it. But since he's so persistent, I must handle this right here and now, and shut it down.

He walks up and casually slides his hands into his suit pants pockets. "Lady Boss tells me to come, I come."

"Look, I'm flattered. But I get to decide who I want and who I don't. Your superhuman level of confidence won't win the girl this time, got it? I'm not interested!"

A grin flashes. "You're not? You sure about that?"

"Very sure."

I freeze as he steps closer to me, very slowly leans in and whispers into the sensitive shell of my ear, "I'm not interested in you either, Meagan." Shivers breeze down my side as I breathe him in. He lingers here and I feel my phone being slipped out of my hand.

"Give that back!"

From under dark eyebrows he glances up at me, swipes it open, types something in, and hands it back. "Call me," he smirks.

I stare after Jeremy as he strolls away headed for the exit. He rakes his fingers through his hair, spins around, walks backward two steps, nods to me, then spins around again and is gone.

Like a mummy I walk out from the server station.

"Ms. Forrester?"

Glancing over I discover I'm face-to-face with Kenny Lively, the restaurant critic. An immediate smile gets plastered on my face. "Mr. Lively! Are you having an enjoyable evening?"

"I am. What was that man's name, the one you were just talking to?"

You never argue or ask why, to a food critic. You just give them anything they want. "That was Jeremy Cocker. He's Senator Justin Cocker's brother."

The critic's salt and pepper eyebrows fly up. "Really? How interesting. He sure can make a drink. The female bartender wasn't nearly as skilled. But don't worry! I won't mention that. He deserves all the accolades I'll give. In fact, I'd recommend you have him teach the others as soon as possible. That man has a gift."

Not wanting to sound like I have no idea what the heck he's talking about, I smile and nod. "Great idea, Mr. Lively. I'll be sure to tell Bryan."

"Good. Fantastic party." He returns to his friends and I head to the kitchen to decipher that bizarre exchange. Remembering my phone I lift it up and read what thick fingers and a smirk just typed:

Free any day of the week. Schedule away…Boss.

And then his phone number.

"What the fuck," I mutter. Bryan strolls into the kitchen, beaming from the success of the evening. "You didn't hire any new bartenders, did you?"

"What are you blathering about?"

"Did you hire Jeremy Cocker as bartender? Because that is the worst idea I've ever heard of, Bryan. You didn't seriously do that, did you?"

Bryan's eyes glaze over and his tone becomes cold and detached. "Are you going to tell me how to run my restaurant?"

"No, I—"

"—You don't want me to second guess hiring you, do you?"

"What? No, I—"

"Can't you see I'm busy?" His voice rises. "Or are you so self-involved that you can't see I'm launching a fucking restaurant here?!"

My mouth slams shut and I hold up a hand in surrender, flipping on my heel.

God, I hate being talked to like that. All the chefs were watching. I'm mortified but I have to get to the bottom of this. Did he hire Jeremy? If I'm not going to get any answers from him I'll get them from Ty.

Smiling at guests waiting to order drinks, I step behind the bar and sidle up to him, asking out of the corner of my mouth in a very quiet voice, "Did Bryan hire a bartender tonight?"

Uncorking a bottle of red wine, Ty grumbles, "Some show-off came back here and took over. I was totally handling it but he pushed me aside. Fuckin' dick."

"What'd he look like?"

"Like an asshole."

"You're not helping." I abandon him for the next bartender, Cathy. She's shaking up a martini when she spots me. "What happened?"

Reliable, intelligent and despite what the critic said about her, she's good at her job. Lowering her voice Cathy confides, "Ty was losing it. One of the guests was pissed, almost lost her mind and was going to complain to you, I'm sure, but then this gorgeous guy jumped back here, flirted with her, made her a hell of a drink and changed the whole dynamic. Bryan saw it, told him to make drinks for the next guys who just happened to be Kenny Lively and his cohorts." Her eyebrows go up as she and I both register the gamble that was. "He aced it, Meagan."

"Where was I during all of this?"

"It happened quickly. One minute I look over and see Ty cracking. The next, stud monster is saving the day with

Bryan and Bon Appétit as his audience." Cathy pauses for effect so this can sink in. "Bryan hired him on the spot. And I hate to say it, but you know what my prediction is?"

I take a not-so-wild guess. "This will be Ty's last night."

"Yup," She pours her shaker's contents into a martini glass and throws a sprig of mint in.

My mind is reeling with this new intel, but the chilled glass caught my eye. "That's a great idea. You weren't doing that at the dry run."

She shrugs, "I saw the new guy do it."

"Not you, too?" I mutter, heading out as she quizzically watches me.

How has Jeremy Cocker managed to charm everyone while I wasn't looking?

So I was wrong in thinking he was coming onto me, but he certainly led me to believe it. Or, did he? Was that all just in my head? One thing I know? Working with him is going to be hell.

14

MEAGAN

Kicking off these heels I set my keys down on the accent table by the front door of my one-bedroom condo. As part of my nightly ritual I trace my fingertips lightly atop a framed picture of my brother Devin with his dog, lingering with a grief-filled tug at my heart.

"Miss you."

I pad into the luxurious comfort of my living room, eager for the feeling of home after a rough night.

I took a lot of care in creating a sanctuary I could lean into when a stressful day threatened to take me to my knees. I want to tuck myself into the tufted couch with some tea, and call my sister for some love.

I roll my eyes at the sink full of dishes and say, deadpan, "You guys'll have to wait."

Grabbing a jam-filled wedge of Brie from the fridge, I slip it onto a small metal platter to soften in the toaster oven while I gather gluten-free crackers, a chamomile teabag, and my favorite mug, turning the kettle on to slowly come to a boil.

"One day I'll have my own grand opening," I whisper to my hot pink orchid petals, touching their silkiness and allowing the evening to wash off of my soul. "And when I do I'm going to recycle. Can you believe he shot that idea down? Of all things to make a stand about."

With my little snack, my phone, and a delicious smelling cup of tea I crawl onto the couch and pick up last month's copy of Bon Appétit, looking for the article Kenny Lively writes so I can get a feel for what he might say about us. In between bites of cheese I mutter to myself, "Hmm, he's got a sense of humor, so that's nice."

A text beep comes through. With my head still buried in the article I reach for my phone and hold it, forgetting to check it because I'm so absorbed in Kenny's descriptive words. Fifteen minutes of reading other food articles later, the phone rings.

I answer, "Hello," distracted.

"You didn't answer my text."

Blinking away from the magazine, I tell Bryan, "Oh, sorry, I was reading and I disappeared for a little while."

"Are you telling me you saw my text and didn't answer?!"

"No, I didn't see it," I hastily say. Which is true. I heard it, but I never looked at it. "Sorry. Won't happen again. What's up?"

"Come over."

Neither of us knows what to do with my delayed response.

After a moment of silence, he asks, "You there?"

"I'm here."

"You're mad at me," he exhales, sounding more human than usual.

"I'm just tired." After hearing this lame excuse, I correct myself, "No, it's not that. I can't just flip the switch like you can."

"What are you talking about? We do this all the time."

Not all the time. We do it rarely. And whenever you want to.

Tucking my feet underneath me I uneasily explain, "No, we work during the days together and often you're not even there when I'm working at your desk doing administrative work, and then later at night you'll call or text me, sometimes, and I'll come over."

"What's the fucking difference?" he grumbles.

"There's a space of time between, where I'm able to separate work from…play. And tonight was all work, a very heavy and important night, and to come over now when I know you don't want anything serious and probably won't even ask me to spend the night, well, I just don't feel up to that right now."

And…inwardly exhale.

Wow.

That took a lot of courage.

Is that how I've been secretly feeling? I wasn't even aware that our unspoken arrangement bothered me until that came tumbling out.

There's a charged silence on the other end of the line, but I keep my mouth shut.

Is he ever going to speak?

Biting my lip I wait.

Did he hang up?

I think he might be waiting for me to cave in. Thinking that maybe I'll get nervous my job is at stake and then say, *okay, I'll come over*. But the idea of driving to his house right now and having him inside me isn't remotely as appetizing as this Brie. In fact, I know I'd be disappointed. You can't reheat this stuff and have it taste as good the second time.

Finally he grumbles, "Suit yourself."

"I'll see you tomorrow, Bryan."

He hangs up. I roll myself into a ball and start rocking, taking deep breaths. My fingers are shaky as I speed-dial Cecily. After three rings I hear her sleepy voice. "Meagan?"

"Hi," I whisper.

"You okay?"

"No. Yes. I don't know. Maybe? I'm just…I'm not happy, Cess."

I can hear the bed shifting under her as she sits up. "Hang on, I'm going downstairs. Just stay there, okay? Have to get my slippers on."

"Thank you," I whisper.

In no time at all her voice is much more alert. "Alright, I'm here."

"You on the couch?"

"Yeah, why?"

"You have grandma's crocheted blanket?"

"Hang on."

I have a hot pink one, she a yellow one, since those have been our favorite colors since we were little, even before Grandma Marnie gave us these one Christmas. She'd made them herself and while the knots aren't perfect, they were looped and cinched with love. My older sister was in high school in her 'have to be cool' stage, but she fell to pieces with gratitude when we unwrapped them. Devin got one, too, his dark blue. Cecily has it tucked away in a wooden box where it doesn't tear our hearts out.

"Okay, I'm wrapped up in it," my sister says.

"Me too. All cozy."

"So, what's going on, kid?"

Biting my lip, I whisper, "Tonight was hard."

"The opening? When you get your own place, it'll be hard then, too."

"I'll be making the calls then. I won't have to second guess my decisions."

"Oh, honey, you'll probably second guess them then, too."

"You know I won't. Sure I might learn from them, but I always trust my gut the first time."

Cecily's patient with me, her voice gentle as she explains, "This is good experience for you so that one day you can avoid making avoidable mistakes."

"We had a hostess tonight who got drunk!"

"Oh no! Does she have a problem?"

"She has to. I smelled alcohol on her during two of the training days and I mistakenly diagnosed it as a hangover but now I think she was drinking during them, and they began at eight in the morning!"

"How sad. But if she does, you know she can't help it. Be firm but kind to her."

"Well, I got one out of two right. And guess which. If we keep her on I'll try and be gentler, but I was so angry! Tonight was crucial!"

"Honey, if she's an alcoholic it doesn't matter how

crucial the day or not, she will drink."

Sighing I mutter, "And Cess, I don't want to go over to his house right now, but part of me is saying I should."

My sister's tone changes immediately to one of warning. "I thought you stopped sleeping with him last month."

"Yeah, well, that didn't stick."

"Meagan," she groans. "If you keep giving it away!"

"He won't buy it, I know. That's why I said no. And I'm also tired of how he speaks to me."

"You know how I feel about that! But do you listen, no. Maybe this will be the last time. He asked you over?"

"Yes. And I was eating the most delicious cheese from Florence, Italy, and now it's gone to waste because I've lost my appetite."

"Eat the cheese and throw the casual sex in the trash. I know it's hard. It's too lonely in your place."

God, that hurt to hear, so like any self-respecting, warm-blooded woman would, I lie through my teeth, "I'm not lonely. I have my work. It's all I need."

"You don't want a happy relationship?"

Biting a cracker I mutter, "I guess I want it all."

"You deserve it all. But only a good man will give it to you."

"There are none left."

She lets out a different kind of sigh that lets me know her patience is disappearing. "You've always had a thing for unavailable men."

On a deep and wonderful stretch of my legs I ask her, "What's wrong with that? Who doesn't love a challenge?"

Kevin's distant crying begins, as if he wants to save his mother from strangling his aunt's neck. "Oh, hon, I've gotta go. He just woke up. Poor li'l guy caught the sniffles at a play date."

"Awwww, how cute is that?"

I can hear her smiling as she quickly says, "I took so many pictures! They were adorable. You okay?"

"I'm better now. I was about to cave and go over."

"Do not do that!"

"I won't. Go get Kev. I love you."

"I love you, too. Don't go over. Sleep in your bed. I'm calling in the morning to check."

"I'm hanging up now!"

"Bye!"

The line goes dead. After a moment of staring at my cheese and crackers, I mumble to it, "I'm not going to eat you. Guess you got lucky. I sure didn't."

15

JEREMY

6:00 A.M. sharp I get a text from my new lady boss that makes me jump out of bed, fully alert and ready for battle.

All last night I waited for a text about my schedule and didn't hear from her. I began to believe she'd talked Marchand out of hiring me and I didn't like that idea at all. I became certain she'd told him about our phone call and he'd nixed the job offer, and neither of them were going to let me know. Strange being worried about something like this. But going back to days filled with nothing brought on a depression I couldn't shake. Fell asleep in dread. Had a dream I was trapped under dead bodies. They became zombies. The worst part was they weren't strangers.

"Shake it off, Jeremy. You're okay."

Be at the restaurant at half past eight to learn the computer. Meagan.

Aslan's head pops up from the foot of the bed. He sees me sliding on my sweats and hoodie, and his massive frame clamors down, huge paws thudding onto the carpet two at a time.

Slap the leash on his chain and we're off and running.

Fucking nightmares. When are they going to end? The war against my demons is worse than any on a battlefield because the fighting never stops.

My head thinks I'm in danger.

And in a way, I am…if I believe it.

So I run.

Get into my body. The tangible. The touch. The real. Everything else is illusion.

The past isn't happening.

The future is a fantasy.

The only thing real is the present.

When we get home Aslan makes a beeline for his water dish as soon as I open the front door. I follow him, panting just as hard as he is, and swing the fridge open for my Britta pitcher. Jake got me into this, years ago. There were so many times I had rank water when I was overseas that this is the one luxury I cared about, the only thing I looked forward to buying. Got a shit-ton of extra filters so I'd never run out. I may have gone overboard.

Picking up my phone I find another text from Meagan.

Did you get my text?

"Shit," I mutter, realizing I should have replied.

Any normal person would have known to do that.

Typing quickly I send her one word:

Done.

Staring at it, I wait. She immediately replies back.

What the hell does that mean? Done?

"Well shit," I grumble, irritated with my lack of communication skills.

I want this job. Can't fuck it up.

I text her:

Done means I'm in. I'll be there. See you soon.

I wait for a response and five minutes later decide none is en route. Tossing the phone onto my couch on the way to the bathroom I walk my sweaty body into the shower and turn up the heat. "Fuck that feels good."

Let it wash over everything.

Take the nightmares away.

Today I soap up like I did when there was a line waiting.

While rubbing the insides of my ears with my towel, I open the door and hurry to my closet. Glancing to Aslan, I ask, "What were they wearing last night?" He lumbers onto his half-crushed dog bed in the corner of my room, staring at me. "All black, right? Safe bet."

I've got Jake's black suit slacks from last night. I give 'em a sniff, mumble, "These'll do," and search for a shirt. The only one I've got is a black tank top. I toss it in the air and catch it before sliding it on.

Padding out to my phone I call my brother. Jake answers right away like he was waiting for my call. "Hey. How'd it go?"

"Good. Might have to get you a new pair of shoes though. The suit should take the wear, but jury's still out."

He chuckles, thinking I got into trouble or something. "Oh yeah? What'd you do?"

"Don't tell the whole family?"

"Of course. You okay?"

"I got a job. Bartending. New restaurant. It's no big deal. Need black shoes today, so I'm using yours."

"Holy shit, Jeremy, that's great!" I hit the speaker button and start putting on my socks because I can tell he's going to give me a speech. "I remember when you bartended. You rocked that shit! And you loved it, right? This is the best news, man. I'm so fuckin' happy for you. We've been worried. All of us. How'd it happen? Wait…I'm confused. You applied for a job last night? That's why you needed the suit? Thought it had something to do with a girl."

"Not exactly," I smirk as I shove his dress shoes on.

"Then what?"

"Look, don't tell the family yet. It might not work out."

"I already said I wouldn't. I won't tell anybody. I just want you happy, man. We all do."

"I know." I take the phone off speaker to bring it to my ear. "I was at a grand opening last night and some dweeb couldn't hack the stress when he was four deep at the bar. I jumped back there to stop the bleeding, and the owner happened to see me at work. Offered me a job. No big deal."

Jake can tell I don't want to get my hopes up. He forces a casual tone. "That's awesome. Take my shoes. Have fun. Let me know how it goes."

"You won't tell anyone?"

"Nope."

"Justin knows."

"What the fuck!?" I start cracking up. "Seriously, Jeremy, what the fuck!?"

"He was at the event. It wasn't planned. Don't be jealous."

Jake mutters, "I'm not jealous."

"Yeah you are. Pussy. I'll call you later."

I hang up on him swearing under his breath.

Quick brush of the teeth and I kneel down to be at my best friend's eye-level. "Hey Aslan, I've got someplace to be for a couple hours. Maybe a few. I don't know. You guard the fortress, okay?"

Poor guy's staring at me like I'm never coming home.

I give his generous neck a hug. "Love ya, buddy. You're in command while I'm gone."

Snatching up my keys I head out.

16

MEAGAN

As the Lyft driver pulls up to the restaurant, golden morning sunlight steams in and illuminates the beauty of Le Marchand's decor. Today I feel as good as that view looks.

I slept as though I had no problems. Passed out as soon as I sunk into my cozy bed, and didn't wake up once before the alarm did its job. The stretch I enjoyed after I silenced the ring felt amazing.

What the hell?

It's only seven-thirty.

What is Jeremy doing here?

"Thank you," I tell the Lyft driver, gathering my purse, eyes darting over to drink in our new employee's attire. He's leaning against a stone wall beneath the restaurant's name, his face down as he reads something on his phone, muscles rippling on his right arm as he swipes the screen with his thumb and frowns in concentration.

I call out, "A tank top? Really?"

His eyes meet mine from under his brow. "Too sexy?"

Sighing I shut the car door and pull my huge ring of keys out. There are ones to my sister and parents' house, Bryan's house, his storage unit, the restaurant, the safe, the back door, and to my house and garage. In between searching for the right one I glance to Jeremy. "You're early."

"I didn't want to be late."

"Well you overachieved that goal," I mutter, sliding the correct key into the lock. "Cathy isn't here yet, so I guess you'll have to wait a whole hour for her to arrive."

He follows me in. We look at each other and I sigh, heading off. His chuckle behind me whips me around to walk backwards with my arms flying up. "What?!"

"Just happy to be here," he smiles.

My head cocks as I try to decide if he meant that or was being sarcastic. I really can't tell with this guy.

"You know what, Jeremy? I was having a great morning until five minutes ago." Stopping in the center of a dozen clean and empty tables I point to a corner of the room. "Why don't you sit at that booth and wait for Cathy. If you stay out of my way we'll get along just fine…ish."

"Fine-ish?" he asks with raised eyebrows.

"Yes."

"We can't be friends?"

"Do you always irritate your friends?"

A grin flashes as he glances away to hide it, raking his right hand through his thick, dark hair. The tank top is tucked into his slacks, but there's no belt. He doesn't need one. Those pants fit his narrow waist and flat stomach perfectly. "Sorry Boss. I was just being me." Jeremy looks up with sincerity in his eyes. "I'll knock it off. I want this. So if you tell me to sit in that booth, then that's where I'll be."

His mask came down so quickly it's jarring. We stare at each other for a few seconds as I sink into the depth of his compelling gaze. What's his story? There's something underneath those looks that I can't put my finger on. Has he had a hard life?

I blink away from him. "Great. Thank you."

I'd planned on being here early so I could enjoy the quiet and some alone-time, get grunt work out of the way in order to enjoy a lazy Sunday afternoon at home before I have to be back here tonight for the real grand opening, the one meant for the public.

We were originally going to be closed on Sundays but Bryan decided the weekends were too lucrative to shut down.

This is the only day of the week when my heart craves being lazy. And I think our employees would be happier and no one would fault us.

"They're not 'our' employees though, are they,

Meagan?" I mutter under my breath while answering email in the back office. "Nope. It's not your call. Nothing is your call."

Did I forget to drink coffee today?

No, I couldn't have.

Holy crap I forgot.

Hitting send I rise, stretch, glancing at the clock. It's been a half hour already?

Heading into the dining room for the server station that houses our industrial sized espresso machine, I stop and peek in first, but discover the booth empty. Scanning the restaurant for Jeremy I spy the top of his head behind the bar.

In order to catch him in the act of who knows what, I tiptoe over. He's squatting in front of bottles, pointing between this one and that, saying aloud, "Okay, so vodkas are to the left, premiums mixed in. Have to fix that. Separate them. Give them distinction. Gins are behind vodka. Remember Bombay Sapphire is on the far end, for now."

Squatting and hunched, the broad expanse of his back is spread wide, every rippling muscle visible under that strip of black cloth he calls a work shirt. In an effort to make myself known I clear my throat. He shoots up about three feet as if a bomb went off by his ear, eyes sharpened with a fight behind them.

My hands fly up as I cry out, "Whoa! It's just me!" He doesn't relax so I take a step behind the bar with him and soften my voice. "Hey, Jeremy, I'm sorry. I really didn't mean to scare you. Truly."

He stares at me, his wall up. "You didn't."

"I tiptoed."

"Why?"

Guiltily I admit, "I thought you were up to something weird."

He glances around the bar. "Like what? Chasing cockroaches to keep them as pets?"

I burst out laughing from nervousness. "No! What? No!! That's definitely not what I was thinking."

"Thought I might as well make use of idle time while I was here."

"I saw that. Impressive." His friendly, goofing-around nature has been replaced by something darker. He really didn't like me sneaking up on him. "I was just going to make coffee. You want some?"

He blinks a moment like he's trying to regain a sense of where he is. Raking a hand though his hair, he nods, eyes falling toward the ground.

"Sure. Yeah. I could use a cup."

"Great, it's this way."

The restaurant is quiet except for our footsteps. I feel

like I did something wrong, worse than just sneaking up on him. To lighten the air with casual conversation I look over my shoulder and see his eyes dart up from my ass. A pulse begins in my core. "Were you just checking me out?"

"Sorry, Boss."

"You were."

"I was. I'm not denying it."

My eyebrows twist and I wring my hands, suddenly very aware of my body, which is a new sensation in this work environment. It's normally formal and all business. Bryan never gives away our nighttime entanglements when I'm on the clock. He never compliments me, checks me out, brushes against me suggestively, none of it. I get texts after I clock out, but I feel almost androgynous when I'm working, except for right now.

Now I feel very much like a woman.

"I'm having a latte."

"Sounds good to me. Teach me how to make it."

Nodding I very self-consciously walk up to the machine. "Here it is."

"Top of the line."

"Bryan likes it that way. Everything has to be the best."

Jeremy slides his hands in his pockets and holds my eyes. "It shows."

My lips part. It felt like he included me, personally, in that. Nervously I ask him, "So I hear you have five brothers? Tell me about them."

"You hear that? From who?"

"People talk."

Jeremy pulls down two, pristine, white mugs for us, his eyes on me while I push the button to ground Sumatra beans and start the lesson. As I teach him our two subjects overlap.

"I'm the youngest of six brothers. All very different, good men."

"You pour the fresh grounds here then compress them with this."

"By the time I got to school they'd done everything there was to be done. I walked onto campuses with a reputation before anyone even knew me."

"Push the double button here and it'll pour into both cups. Or press this one if you're making only one and position your cup accordingly." I meet his eyes and he nods.

"At first it was easy. Piece of cake to walk in the grooves they all made. But then I started to ask, who am I? How am I my own man?"

"And you were what age?"

"Fourteen."

On a smile I tease him, "Fourteen and already thinking you were a man?"

His face is sober. "My dad raised us to be men. None of us stayed a boy long. We were all the same in that, strong, loyal, true to ourselves and what we believed in. Men."

"I see."

"But I didn't have a sense of who I was to become. How I'd spend my time. What made me happy. What made me different. How I was going to leave my mark."

Jeremy inhales and glances away, then back to me, holding my eyes. He's open, the wall down, the joking abandoned. I can't stop staring at him.

"Go on."

"I didn't have a purpose. I didn't know how I was going to make my mark in the world and not just be their little brother."

My voice is soft as I ask, "Have you found it?"

He holds my look a moment. "I don't know. So, what next?"

"With?"

"With the lattes."

"Oh!" Turning to the espresso-filled mugs I struggle to remember the next step. Reaching into the small refrigerator below I grab whole milk and smile at Jeremy, "Would you hand me that silver steamer?"

"This little pitcher thing?" He points at it.

"Yes."

"Here ya go, Boss." The sides of our hands touch and a spark of electricity makes us jump. "Whoa!"

"Ha!" he laughs.

"I guess the rug…"

"Yeah."

As I stare at him his eyes darken.

"Um, so, you fill the pitcher halfway with milk, like this. Place it under the white steamer spigot thingy. I don't know what it's called. Then roll the spigot around in the milk, hover it just under the surface to make it foam. See?"

"Let me try," Jeremy murmurs, coming up behind me. I freeze as his large, warm hands wrap around mine as I roll the pitcher around.

He takes control and adds pressure to my stunned fingers. "Like this?" he whispers in my ear. Our bodies are touching and mine just caught fire, humming, heat pooling between my thighs and trailing in every direction. My eyelids close as I start to lean into him against my will.

The front door opens in the distance. Jeremy smoothly steps away from me, releasing my hands in a hurry.

Cathy calls out, "Meagan?"

My voice cracks, "Over here!" Glancing to him over my shoulder I pour the perfect foam into our cups. "Cathy will be training you so, now that you know how to make lattes, go with her to the bar."

"You got it." He smiles as if nothing just happened between us, but as he goes to leave he lays his hand on the wall, meets my eyes and confesses, "I already knew how to make lattes. They're not a new invention."

He winks and disappears as my jaw drops.

17

JEREMY

While I love getting a rise out of Meagan this time I got a rise out of me. The wrong kind. The tent-in-my-borrowed-black-slacks kind. "Hey Cathy, I'm hitting the head then I'll be right over."

"Okay!" she calls out on her way to the bar in a halter and black jeans that make my eyebrows twitch.

Wasn't I chastised for this shirt?

Whatever.

Pacing in the men's room I roll over in my mind what just went down. She could have pushed me away, but she leaned into me a little.

Or was that me leaning in?

The chemistry started having a mind of its own. Another second and I don't know what would have happened.

Grabbing onto the sleek edges of a sink I lock eyes

with my reflection. "Are you done self-sabotaging? Trying to get fired? You saw the texts. She's involved with the boss. Don't fuck this up!"

Splashing cold water on my face, I snatch a paper towel and rub my skin, soaking up and tossing the sweat from my mistake in the trash.

As I stroll out to the bar with my zipper flat again, I smile at my new co-worker, "Ready to learn whatever you've got to teach. I'm Jeremy."

"Cathy." She's slicing limes, her pretty head tipped down but her eyes on me. "I see you didn't get the memo either."

"What memo?"

"Not to wear a tank," she smiles while snapping her halter top's spaghetti strap. Her large breasts bounce under the gesture and I force myself not to glance down.

It's not easy being a guy. Not the slightest bit easy. Cathy's flirting, and it's intentional. I've been on the receiving end my whole life.

I'm not into her and I hope she cuts it out because I have a sneaking hunch if she doesn't, my lady boss will increase the verbal attacks. Walking behind the bar I tell Cathy, "I'm going shopping later today. So what about these computers?"

She drops the limes while I wait, licks her fingers,

staring at me, then smiles as she washes them off in the sink with soap, taking extra long with the suds and massaging. By the way, her ass is in the air. Fuckin' hell.

Meagan walks up, coffee in hand. She'd come out from the kitchen, where I'm guessing the office is. She caught me looking where I wasn't supposed to. Her blue eyes sharpen like I'm the biggest man-whore. She darts an irritated glance to Cathy's backside, rolls her eyes and disappears.

Under my breath, I mutter, "Great."

"What?" Cathy asks, straightening and sweeping her hair back.

"Great," I smile. "Can't wait to get started."

"You were really impressive with those cocktails you made."

"Thanks."

She crooks a finger at me. "C'mere."

I hesitate but when she walks to the iPad I cross to her, all ears. "I saw these last night. We use iPads?" Feels so weird to say we, like I'm one of them now.

"Yep. There are two, and some nights there will be three of us tending bar. But I hope they let us run some night with only two because, you know, more money," she smiles, touching the screen with sensual slowness, her tits pushed out. "The servers have iPhones on the floor." She may as well have said, *lay me on the floor*. "The ability to make calls has been disabled. It's just Wi-fi for our restaurant system's app. Isn't that hot?"

I swallow hard. "Yep."

"I think so, too." Her eyelashes drop as she gazes at my mouth. "That's how they put in their orders. See the printer at the end?" She points and then runs a hand through her sweet-smelling hair as she looks at me from over her shoulder.

"Yep. I see it."

"Whoever's manning that side will make the server's drinks. The orders print out from there." She walks to it, bends over in front of a storage cabinet, ass high like a cat's. "Extra paper is in here." She shoots up, flips her hair back in the sexiest way. "You've used that system before, right?"

"Yeah. I just need to learn the computers. The rest I can do on my own."

Cathy saunters back to me and leans against the counter. She touches my arm and whispers on a sensual smile, "You don't need anyone to show you around?"

"I've already shown myself around."

"Cocky, aren't you?"

"Nah, just…"

"Cocky," she finishes. "I know your kind. Oh, don't get that face. I've got a boyfriend. I'm not hitting on you." My eyebrows fly up, and she laughs. The flirtation drops and she eyes me with a sharp intelligence that wasn't evident a moment ago. With a strong voice that's all business she informs me, "I'm just showing you, bottle flipper, that while your drink-making skills might've put you in Bryan's spotlight, I have skills of my own that will get tips, so don't underestimate me."

I break into a grin. "Hilarious."

She gives me another wink. "Gotcha, didn't I?"

"You certainly did."

"Now let's get to work."

We go over the menu items, where to ring up well, call and premium liquors, how to log a free drink so the inventory is accounted for. Sometimes you have to buy a drink, or a round, for guests to keep them feeling special, or to fix an error and keep them coming back.

"He's been in the business for twenty years after all," she explains with respect.

"How old is he?"

Cathy likes to spin the ring on her index finger around when she thinks. She's done this at least five times in the last two hours. "Almost forty, I think."

I expected a lower number. Maybe thirty-two or three.

She reads my mind. "He looks good, doesn't he?"

"I'm into him," I smirk, and she laughs.

"Yes, sure you are."

Meagan walks out of the kitchen and glances between us. Her hair looks freshly combed and her lipstick has just been reapplied. "What's funny?" Her eyes rest on me as she waits for the answer. It's so fucking hard not to ask if she flossed, too.

"Nothing," I shrug.

Cathy leans against the counter. "Just getting to know each other."

Caramel brown eyes flicker as her neck lengthens and she exits, footsteps fading as she heads into the office. It takes me a second to turn back to my trainer and when I do, she's watching me.

"Meagan's with Bryan."

My head goes back as I shove my hands into my pockets. "So?"

With a knowing smile she turns the iPad off. "You're all set. Go memorize the menu. If guests ask about the food you need to know the answers. When's your first shift?"

"Let me go check." I start to leave but see her smile. "Stop looking at me like that. I'm just going to ask the boss when I work."

Cathy smirks, "You'd better be."

18

MEAGAN

I'm re-reading the report from last night to make sure I ordered everything that needs replenishing after last night's event.

Jeremy's deep voice interrupts with, "Busy, Boss?"

Surprised goosebumps spring up on my skin and I glance over to find him leaning on the doorframe.

"Yes, I'm busy. What is it?"

"Just want to know when I'm working."

"Oh." My eyelashes flutter to the keyboard and I do a search for our calendar. "You're replacing Ty so you're on tonight, Tuesday and Wednesday." Our eyes meet as I ask, "You all done out there?"

"Think so. I'll go home and memorize the menu. Buy some work clothes. What time you want me back here tonight?"

"Five."

Bryan's voice booms through the empty kitchen, bouncing off the metal shelves, stoves and pots and pans, giving him the quality of someone talking in a stadium. "How's my apprentice doing today?"

I straighten in my chair. My eyes flit to Jeremy and he straightens up, too. Bryan walks past him, glances up and down his attire and says with disdain, "If you're working for me you'll wear a real shirt."

Losing none of his confidence Jeremy says, "I'm shopping this afternoon."

Bryan locks on me. "What's going on here?"

My fingers jet toward the screen. "You want to give him Ty's schedule right?"

The tightness around his lips and eyes relax.

Was he jealous of us being back here alone?

It looked that way.

Leaning in to read the schedule Bryan touches my shoulder and holds there. This is new. "Ty was on tonight? Hmmm." He rubs my shoulder before straightening up and turning to Jeremy. "Let's see how you do this evening. If you're as good as yesterday I'll give you weekend shifts. Don't fuck this up."

Jeremy's eyes shine with the challenge. "Works for me."

"Go buy a uniform that's not inspired by gay bars."

133

Bryan turns his back on him. It's how he dismisses everyone. I glance to Jeremy. His eyes darken before he disappears.

"Is everything ready?"

"For tonight, absolutely. I called Smith's and they're making a special run so we have the arugula, cabbage, kale…"

Leaning against the wall Bryan waves me into silence. "Yes, yes, don't list them all to me. Jesus. Did you order everything we need or not?"

"I did."

"Why didn't you come over last night?"

I stare at him. "You're going to bring that up now?"

"Why wouldn't I?"

"I thought we don't mix business with…whatever it is we're doing."

With a volcano brewing behind his eyes he ignores this and waits for an answer to his question.

Nervous he might blow up I hastily explain, "I was tired. It was a very big night, and my head hasn't completely healed yet, either." I point to my bandage.

"Doesn't look that bad to me."

The sounds of staff members walking into the kitchen distract us both, thank God. Bryan pushes off the wall and strolls out of the office just like that.

I call his name and he pokes his head back in. "Yes?"

"Is there a chance I can get behind the line tonight? I'd like to cook."

He makes a face. "Who would watch the floor? I need you out there. This is the official opening night. For the common people."

"I want to cook! I'm a chef. I went to culinary school." I stare at him hoping he can hear how much I mean it. "When are you going to give me a chance?"

Bryan smiles that charismatic smile of his. "Meagan, you will have your chance soon. Didn't you see Karate Kid?"

I relax a little. "Of course."

He walks in and touches my cheek. "Then you know why I'm doing this to you. Paint the fence, wax the cars. Learn to have a little patience." He leans down and kisses my forehead, directly on my stitches. I hide that it hurts. From the kitchen Alberto calls his name and suddenly I'm alone in the office.

That made me feel better. I'm very glad I asked. I've been so confused as to why I'm called his apprentice when I'm receiving no hands-on culinary training.

Okay, so this menial crap isn't for nothing.

I'm working *toward* something. This has been like a test and one day very soon I will be standing behind those stoves with a row of perfectly aligned plates laid out before me full of food I created that complete strangers I will never meet are about to enjoy.

I cannot wait!

Turning back to the computer I double check the ingredients while running my finger down the screen. To make sure I show that man my worth I will make no mistakes.

The sound of the cooks laughing grabs my attention. They're having so much fun I rise to peek out and see what so funny.

Bryan is teaching them a new dish he's just dreamed up for tonight's special. They are laughing out of camaraderie. Bryan catches me and waves me back into the office. "Wait your turn," he smiles.

A couple of the other men turn around to see me. The look in their eyes…it's like they're better than me. Is that just my imagination?

Carlo can't cook his way out of a McDonald's kitchen. I tasted his work. He over-salts.

Biting my tongue I disappear into the office, keeping the door open. I want to hear the cooking lesson even if I can't see it.

The hardest test is learning to put my ego aside.

19

MEAGAN

I'm so busy monitoring the little things, from the bathrooms staying clean, to helping the valets adjust how they organize car fobs, to accepting the late delivery of an industrial sized box of Panko breadcrumbs from the service door just in time for a big order, that I'm hardly on the floor during the first two hours we're open.

Finally I have a chance to stroll through the main dining room and greet guests, see how they're doing, and make sure everything is running smoothly.

"Oh, it's delicious!" "Wonderful!" "Incredible!" "And I love these little spoons!" These are some of the raving compliments I hear as I walk from table to table.

Across the crowded room I catch a glimpse of Jeremy Cocker, and pause. He's got the shaker in his hand, rapidly pumping it in the air while he grins at a female guest whose face I can't see. He leans to the side and suddenly a bottle goes flying. He catches it and starts making a drink with one hand while he pours the cocktail from the shaker into a separate glass, with his other. He looks so comfortable that I'm blown away.

He glances over to me, catches me staring, and his smile falters.

But as quickly as we locked eyes he's back to doing his job.

Now I'm curious.

I start making my way to Jeremy. He keeps glancing over and holding my look. He knows I'm coming. His showmanship increases. Cathy is glancing over with jealousy. Lana is at the service station. Since she wasn't here last night, I walk behind the bar and decide to pass by Jeremy and Cathy to see how Lana's doing.

It's a great excuse to spy with.

But when I'm right behind Jeremy he turns around, zips by my body with one arm, grabs a bottle, meets my eyes and says, "Hey there." He tosses the bottle in the air and continues making the cocktail.

That took my breath away, like a bolt of lightning whisked by my side. I step back and watch Jeremy work, forgetting all about Lana.

Crossing my arms in amazement I stare as he makes drink after drink without breaking a sweat, smiling and talking with the guests as easily as if he's known them his whole life.

He charms everyone, even the men. They love the tricks, and his drinks seem to be the best there is. "The perfect balance," I hear a man mumble on his way to a table. I think he came to have Jeremy make his drink, rather than Lana, who's doing all of the floor server's orders tonight.

The women—the way they look at Jeremy—they may as well strip their bras off and toss them at his head.

Bryan appears on the other side of the counter, eyes darting from Jeremy to me. He motions for me to join him, and the two of us walk into the dining room together. "Do you like that boy?" he asks.

Instinct screams that I'm in trouble.

Bryan is considered the best in his field at this very moment. The star of Atlanta. He's flying on a magic carpet.

And there is Jeremy, also skilled. I was watching for too long because I'd never seen anything like it.

But witnessing Bryan Marchand cook ten entrees at once with every one leaving the kitchen at the perfect temp and so amazing you eat past full? That impresses me far more and I want him to know it. Besides, if I bruise his ego I will be on the street, my reputation shot. He is not the type of person to let you go without burning the bridge behind you and smiling as he snuffs out the match.

"I think you misunderstood my watching him, Bryan," I smile as I touch his arm. "I wasn't in awe of him. I was in awe of you, thinking how impressed I was with how smart you are. Jeremy's skills make Le Marchand even better because who else has those tricks? And did you see how the women stared? It's why you hired Mira, because of her looks. He's a perfect replacement for that nerdy little boy. I know I told you it was a bad move to add Jeremy to your roster, but now it's confirmed once again that you're a genius."

Holy shit, I can really pile it on thick, huh?

Bryan's smile returns, now with pride behind it. His suspicion has vanished. Right out here in front of the entire dining room he touches the small of my back, leaning in to whisper in my ear, "You like your men older don't you?"

Happily surprised by the public display of affection I whisper back, "Boys don't know what they're doing. So boring."

He laughs and turns to introduce himself to a table of four. They recognize his famous face in an instant. I stand beside him. But then as the conversation continues and I'm not introduced or addressed, I grow increasingly more awkward. I pull my phone out like I got a text message and start typing away to nobody, quickly exiting the area.

At the server's end of the bar, our voluptuous, raven-haired Lana has drinks lined up in neat rows for the waitstaff.

She's just as attractive as Mira but not nearly as dim. This one is as smart as I am.

"Looks like you found a system."

She throws me a distracted smile. "I had to. It's a mob scene!"

"How are things going with the new guy? He causing you any trouble?"

As she uncaps two beer bottles she shakes her head. "Who, Jeremy? He's awesome! Cathy and I were telling him we hope he gets the weekend shifts with us so he can handle the ladies while we focus on the men." She gives me a look that's all business. "Tips tips tips."

I have nothing else to say. I think I'm just hoping for her to give me more information about him. "You don't think he's obnoxious?"

She glances to Jeremy, her long hair cascading around her shoulders in the process. She whips around to face me again and it does the exact same thing. "I don't know, Meagan, I like that he's a little obnoxious. Show me a meek man and I'll show you a guy who's bad in bed. You've heard about the Cocker boys right?" She chuckles in a sexy way, grabbing a bottle of our best red and setting it on a drink ticket. "I know a few women who've been lucky enough to climb that family tree. More than a few. They all compare their future men to that one night."

I can't help but snort, "One night? Are you saying the Cocker Brothers never come back for seconds?"

"Not that I've ever heard of." She rushes off, grabs a bucket of limes, hurries back and fills up her empty condiment tray. "Look at this! I'm running out. We're selling so much booze tonight."

"I'm still stuck on what you just said. They never spend a second night with women?"

She grins and pulls a fresh drink ticket from the printer. "Except for the women they marry, nope. Maybe that's just a legend. I've never had a chance to try it out. I mean I know of one girl who slept with Jaxson for a couple months, but now she's friends with his wife! Can you believe it? She must be lusting after him every time she comes over for dinner! Oh, and there was that waitress with the Senator. We all know about that."

"Yeah," I mutter. Except for that waitress' story, I'm totally in the dark about the Cocker family, but I want Lana to keep gossiping.

I have no idea who Jaxson is.

Jeremy didn't have time to tell me their names.

And really, all J's?

That's a little ridiculous. Or adorable.

I can't decide which, but I'm holding onto the former for my own sense of sanity. I'm growing interested in Jeremy.

And Lana only makes it worse when she throws this bomb on me:

"And from what I hear, our boy Jeremy is the last single one. Clock's ticking!"

That's what Justin told me last night, too, wasn't it? My mouth slackens as I glance over to where Jeremy is flipping bottles at the far end of the bar like some sort of gorgeous circus performer. He locks eyes with me and gives me a wink, and I clamp my mouth shut.

Lana glances over her shoulder at him, too, her gorgeous black hair fanning out again. Oh, she does that on purpose!

Woman-to-woman she leans in to tell me in a private volume, "I'm going to see if I can't get in there. Oooooh. Just thinking about him naked has me all..." She laughs under her breath and doesn't finish the sentence. Not that anybody needs her to.

"Good luck with that," I mutter.

So he can make a drink.

So his smile is of the panty-dropping variety.

I've seen his apartment.

He's one of those Millennials who can't get his act together because his parents babied him, he was popular in high school, and now thinks he can slide by on his hot looks.

He'll probably fuck up soon and get fired.

143

Once I spend more time with him my stupid little spark of interest will get extinguished. I'm sure the more I get to know him the more bored I'll become.

20

JEREMY

As the last patron tucks his wallet into his back pocket, Lana purrs from my left, "Nice moves."

I'm washing glasses in the sink with suds up my forearms. I glance to her. Oh hell. This is it. Those suggestive smiles she's given me all night are about to ripen into an offer.

"He was going to buy Single Malts for his friends with or without my selling him."

"Not him," she smiles, rolling her eyes like I'm being silly. "You're *good.*"

Shoving two soapy glasses into the rinsing-sink I shrug, "Not my first time."

"Mmm," she hums like I purposefully said a double entendre. I didn't.

Cathy calls over from counting the register, "You make me look bad, standing next to you and your tricks."

I laugh under my breath and keep working.

"Why don't we all go grab a drink after this? Celebrate," Lana smiles, and then whips her hair around to see if Cathy's in. I get a whiff of her shampoo and immediately my muscles tighten. Been a long time since I've been with anyone.

I pick up the condiment tray. "Do we throw these out and start fresh tomorrow?"

Cathy nods and then answers Lana's question. "Can't. My man and I have a date with Netflix tonight." Answering me, she points to the fridge. "The limes, oranges and lemon twists that we cut before the shift, the ones in those big white jugs? They stay put. But the ones that have been sitting out, Bryan wants us to trash them."

"Got it." I walk to the garbage can, my back to the girls.

"What about you, Jeremy?" Lana purrs.

One of the things I don't miss about civilian life is fending off the women. I know most guys would hear me say that and want to punch me out. But fuck it. If you've spent all your school years being chased you start to wonder where the challenge is. You start to take advantage since it's so freely offered. Me and my brothers all went through that stage. For years. When I was twenty-one and bartending at some of the hottest bars in the city, I got my fair share of ass.

It gets old. Empty. Soulless.

Lana here doesn't know me. And we're working together so no matter how good her shampoo smells or how big her rack is, screwing her could royally screw us both if things turned into drama, which they often do with casual sex.

It's just a need to be loved that makes us try the short-term fix of clamping together for a few sweaty minutes.

I get it.

We all have that need to connect. But in a deeper way than just a couple hours can give. Deep down we're all looking for something real, even if we don't want to admit it.

My brothers, for example. Maybe Jason is the only one I can point at and say he hoped to find *the one* ever since he was a kid.

But despite their manwhore ways the others have fallen like domino pieces in an unpredicted tornado. Wedding rings flying on them before they even knew what the fuck happened.

They all must have secretly wanted something real, so when they found it, they locked it down. Claimed it. Wouldn't let it go, and never will. They're going to hang on even when times get rough as they always do because that's just life. The shit's not easy. So you stick together.

I've resisted following my brothers' leads in so many

ways, and while I don't see where I have anything to offer a wife, with my head as fucked as it is, I guess I want that in my future. Somehow.

But it ain't coming from Lana.

And I feel empty enough when I wake up without having some stranger next to me who I don't want to have breakfast with.

She's got, *you're my next conquest* all over her face, and it's got nothing to do with me.

Who I really am.

What I'm made of.

What I can offer.

Lana asks again since I haven't answered her, "What d'ya say, Jeremy? Grab a drink with me."

Meagan walks out of the kitchen just three feet away from where I'm standing. Her soft brown eyes sharpen and flicker from me to Lana, then back to me, before she lifts her head and continues to the front.

She heard that.

Thinks I'll accept.

The girl looks down on me. I can feel it. I find it amusing if not a little strange. Never had anyone shove their nose up in the air around me as much as that girl does. And I sure do love to piss her off.

So I almost agree to the drink. Even open my lips to

say yes. But that would mean I'd have to be alone with Lana. I'm not in the mood.

"I've got to walk my dog," I shrug, strolling back to wash the empty condiment tray and grab a towel to dry it. I can tell she's about to offer to come with me so I quickly add, "And I have plans after that. Otherwise, I would."

"Bummer. Another time."

"Sure."

Lana goes back to her side. The restaurant is empty. Sound travels. I know Meagan was listening. I can see her futzing at the host stand. Maybe she's pretending to work.

I bet it's an act.

I caught her watching me a lot tonight, just itching to fire me, and looking for a way. Well, I won't give her one.

Cathy's voice breaks through the quiet. "You have a dog?"

"Yep. First night I've been away from him this long since I got him."

"Awww, poor guy. He must miss you. What's his name?"

Throwing a towel over my shoulder I say on a smile, "Name's Aslan."

I hear a gasp from the host stand and glance over to see Meagan staring ahead. She looks over her shoulder at me, with a weird expression like I struck a chord.

Raising my voice a little to include her in the conversation, I ask her, "You read the book, Boss?"

She nods, "Yes. When we were kids." Her fingers look a little shaky as she slides the iPad into the drawer and locks it away for the night. I've seen men and women in the Corps with that same dazed look after a major blast has rocked their eardrums to bits.

"Family thing?"

"Sorry," she asks, cocking her head as she walks toward us between the empty dining tables.

"Was it a family tradition, the books? You look like they meant a lot to you."

Like she doesn't want to talk about it, she glances between the three of us and exhales, blinking to clear her eyes. Dismissively she explains, "My mother read them to us, that's all. I just…my mind's on something else."

She passes the bar for the kitchen and I know she's lying. I triggered a past memory. Is her mother dead?

"Hey, you okay?"

She nods and doesn't answer, disappearing.

Cathy meets my eyes and whispers, "What was that about?"

I shrug, "I don't know. She's met my dog. I think it was about the book."

"What book?"

"You haven't read them?" Lana says, her voice also hushed. "Everyone's read them. *The Lion, The Witch and The Wardrobe,* by C.S. Lewis."

"Oh, no, I never did," Cathy says. "You named your dog after them, Jeremy?"

"Yeah. We read them as boys. But my favorite was The Magician's Nephew. In the series Aslan was the name of the lion. It actually means Lion in Turkish."

From the blank look in her eyes, Cathy missed out on one of the best children's books of all time.

21

JEREMY

Lana's ears are perked. "Meagan met your dog?"

"Yep."

Both my co-workers wait for more. I give them a smirk but no explanation. More fun this way.

We all return to cleaning, but now Lana has decided to stop showing me her crack every chance she gets. Guess she thinks Meagan has beaten her to the punch. Fucking hilarious.

Bryan walks in from outside, grinning and looking every bit the owner of this fine dining establishment. He's removed the chef's coat and is strolling around in a suit with his tie undone. I'm pretty sure he's trying to look rakishly godlike. What a douche.

He was a dick to me today, making it clear he's boss and I'd better bow down. I need this job, so I play the game without an ounce of shame.

But I sure as fuck don't like the guy.

As I clean my station I tell him, "People had only good things to say tonight."

"It's true, Bryan," Cathy calls over, shuffling a stack of one dollar bills. "We heard hundreds of gushing compliments tonight, huh, Lana?"

"Oh my God, Bryan, they love everything! Even the bathrooms."

He gives a smile as if he already knows the place is perfect. "Really?"

"Yes!" Lana points to the barstools in front of her. "Three women sitting right here went on and on about the bottle of Chanel's Chance you leave in the ladies bathroom, and all the little toiletries we women might need at a moment's notice. But no bathroom attendant making you feel like you're being watched. They loved it!"

Bryan chuckles under his breath and rakes his hair back again. He locks eyes with me. "I watched you tonight."

I pause. "Hope I impressed."

This is the moment he reveals my fate.

Suddenly I'm breaking a sweat.

My heartbeat starts pounding in my ears.

What the fuck?

You know what it is?

For the first time since I've been back in the states, six

hours in a row passed by completely ghost-free. From when the first guest walked in the door to when the last one left, my head has been right the fuck here in the present moment.

I was smiling.

I was busy with something that made me feel good, not bad.

I had no regrets about anything I did tonight.

I was free.

"I'm happy to be here," I add when he says nothing. He's concentrating on me, not sure if he wants to kick my ass to the curb.

This guy has the key, and he knows it.

He knows he's making me perspire.

Fucking asshole.

He's getting off on it.

I swallow hard but try to hide it.

"I had five separate people compliment me on hiring you."

"Five, huh? That's good to hear."

"Yes…" He waves two fingers in the air and strolls languidly toward the kitchen. Just before he disappears he mutters, "You'll be working weekends."

My lungs release.

That guy just leveled me.

I'm blinking at the floor, near panting. This reaction

has me thunderstruck. It was as if my life depended on him saying I could stay.

Cathy's cautious voice breaks through my stunned haze. "Congratulations, Jeremy."

I glance over to her and mumble, "Thanks."

Under her breath Lana says, "Wow, he really doesn't like you."

My spine stiffens. She gives me a look like I just lucked out. Cathy's eyebrows are up in the exact same way, both in agreement that Bryan almost fired me.

Cathy and I lock eyes. She whispers, "The business man in him couldn't let you go after all the compliments. But be careful."

I nod, "Okay. Thanks."

Cathy is a good woman. Smart. Capable. Honest. I like her. I think I've got a friend in her.

Lana might become one. Who knows? Jury's still out.

We finish shutting the bar down. No casual chatter. Each of us wants to show off our best.

We all felt that heat.

This restaurant is going to blow up. This is just the beginning. It could mean a lot of money for Cathy and Lana.

It could mean sanity for me.

When the ladies are grabbing their purses and putting their jackets on, I offer, "You want me to show you how to spin bottles?"

They both light up.

"Yeah!"

"Hell yes!"

I motion to their stations. "Tighten the plastic wrap on those pour spouts and watch me. You grab the bottle by the top here. Don't do this with full bottles until you're ready. But when they're half full or less they're lighter. As you get good, you can throw any weight with no problem. Grab it here." I wait for them to wrap their hands around their bottle in the right place. "Good. Now you're going to flip your wrist counter-clockwise and up a little, your arm swinging up but not too much. Don't try it yet, and don't think about it when you do. The important thing is *to believe* that you can catch it. Say to yourself right now, *I can catch this every time.*"

"I can catch this every time," they whisper to themselves, eyes focused.

"Say it again."

A little louder they say in unison, "I can catch this every time. I can catch this every time."

"Okay, now watch me first. I'm going to do it twice. Then let go of all thought and fear, and allow your body to copy what it saw me do. Ready?" They nod. I toss the bottle up, watch it spin, and catch it upside, ready to pour. I turn it back upright, then repeat the toss.

"Got that?" They nod, bottles ready. "By osmosis you just learned how. Now trust that you can do it, and do it."

The bottles whip above them, glint in the chandelier's light, and BOOM. They catch them on the first try.

"I did it!" Cathy cries out.

"Me too!!!" Lana grins, eyes wide.

"But it wasn't as smooth as when you do it, Jeremy," Cathy says, shoulders slumping.

"No! Don't start doubting yourself! Let that shit go right now." I point at her. "Hey, you fell the very first time you tried to walk, right? Then you fell every fucking day until you didn't. *Now* how often do you fall? Once a year or something, right?" They both laugh. "I'm serious. Everything takes practice, but if you believe you can do it, you can. Do the work. Keep it up. Enjoy the process and reap all the rewards."

Lana and Cathy are staring at something.

Whipping around I blink a few times at Meagan and Bryan. How long they've been there?

From the look on Lady Boss, she doesn't know what to make of me. And we all know that Bryan isn't my fan.

Sliding my bottle back into the bin I give my best smile. "If we're all back here doing tricks, profits are going to be insane."

Cathy chimes in, "I caught it, Bryan. Want to see?"

She tosses it and while it spins in the air my world slows way the fuck down. If she catches that thing my declaration has merit, and so does employing me.

The restaurant is silent save for the whir of glass on air. She catches it like a pro.

I exhale.

Lana bursts into applause.

Cathy grins to her boss.

"That your second time?" he asks her.

"Ever! Yes! And I caught it the first time, too. Can you believe it?"

His eyes dance with appreciation as those fucking pursed lips of his slide into a smile. "Very nice." He touches Meagan's elbow to guide her away as he says, "Keep practicing. I think you're onto something, Cathy."

Meagan's eyes flit to me.

"Thanks, Bryan!" Cathy calls after him.

I snatch up my keys from their hiding place and toss them in the air. They rattle loudly. Bryan's hand drops to Meagan's lower back. She glances up to him and I can tell by her face that he doesn't normally touch her in public.

He's sending me a message.

As they pass Lana and Cathy both touch my arm, a silent thank you for the lesson.

And a silent apology for its tepid reception.

22

JEREMY

Bryan hasn't touched Meagan all night. It's four weeks since Le Marchand opened and I've learned two very important things:

Meagan wants to be in the kitchen.

Bryan doesn't want her there.

The opposite of most households.

He's holding her back. I think it's wrong, and I hate seeing her work eighty-hour weeks at something she doesn't enjoy. However it's given me insight into who she is to watch her paying her dues like she has been. She's got character, even if she is a hothead. The more I've watched Meagan the more I want to know, and the more I want to protect her.

I Googled him and his achievements. He studied at École de Cuisine Alain Ducasse, supposedly the best culinary school in France. He made waves there, a name for himself, and then moved to New York where he worked his way to head chef at three of the top restaurants. That he's graced Atlanta with his presence is how he looks at this move to the South, but I could give a fuck about what he's achieved.

He looks down his nose at all but the chefs.

I believe that's one reason Meagan is losing control of her patience. She wants to be one so he will start treating her with the same respect he treats them. I've overheard him barking at her. She rarely gives it back but when she does, it's hard for me to hide my laughter.

This 'thing' they have is between them, but I want to butt in anyway. I want to hit the guy so bad I can taste it. And I also want to keep my job.

It's changed my life, I know that. Aslan and I do a normal run in the morning and afternoon before my shift starts, but that's it now. No more five-runs-a-day until I wear the poor guy out.

After our second one I'm itching to get here and do my thing, five nights a week. Sometimes six if somebody agrees to give up their shift, but with the money we make they rarely do no matter how many times I ask.

They think I need the cash. I don't.

When I'm not scheduled I'm jittery and bored out of my fuckin' mind. Will it ever get better? Maybe when I start to believe I'm really done with what I've left behind. The nightmares still come.

Every.

Single.

Fucking.

Night.

As the Friday night crew heads out of the dark restaurant after closing, Bryan and Meagan are not touching or even looking at each other.

His head is in his phone.

She's concentrating on the keys to lock up.

Lana and Cathy say, "Goodnight," and Bryan mutters the same, heading to his car. Alone.

Is he going to ask Meagan to follow?

His steps slow and I lose hope, thinking he's waiting for her. But then he slides his phone into his pocket and walks away without even so much as looking back.

She inserts the key in, and glances over her shoulder to him. Her eyelashes flutter to me, and back to the lock.

I casually stop her. "Oh, I forgot something, Boss. Can you unlock that again? Sorry. I'll run in and be right back."

"Sure, okay," she mumbles from miles away.

Slipping back inside I stroll to the bar, taking my time. I pretend to grab an item, totally faking it, slipping my empty hand in my pocket. Again I take my time walking back.

Meagan's staring at her phone when I appear. I pull my wallet out of my pocket, where it's been the whole time, and show her. "Almost didn't remember this," I smile.

She nods and locks the door with one hand ordering a Lyft on their app.

I glance to the parking lot. His Porsche is gone.

"Save your money. I can give you a ride."

Meagan glances up in surprise. She makes a face. "Let me guess, there's a dead fish on the passenger seat and you want me to sit on it."

On an amused chuckle I ask, "Now why would I leave a dead fish in my car?"

"Off chance I needed a ride."

"That'd be a hell of a gamble. I'd lose either way. You must think I'm pretty devious…or stupid."

She dryly mutters, "Well, not devious," she smiles.

I laugh out loud and she breaks into a grin. God I love making her feel good. "Even a stupid guy knows it's better to catch a ride from someone you know, over having to make idle chit-chat with a stranger when you're tired. It's late. Cancel the ride."

She hesitates but finally closes the app.

Side by side we walk toward my beat-up, second-hand, black Jeep Wrangler, me with my hands in my pockets.

"You'd better not kidnap me and drive me to Florida and make me…"

I cock an eyebrow, waiting for what I'd make her do in

this imaginary scenario.

She glances to me, and stammers, "Drink Mai Tais or something, I don't know!"

"Perish the thought," I sarcastically say. "How could you turn down a vacation and a Mai Tai?"

"If you were making them I wouldn't be able to."

I bump her shoulder with mine. "A compliment? Did hell freeze over today?"

She laughs, "It froze a long time ago. Today it melted. Now you can shake off the ice and walk out of there."

"I thought I wasn't evil?"

"Well, the devil may have you trapped. Who knows?"

Footsteps fall in sync as we don't discuss what she really meant there.

Bryan has us all trapped.

I'm grateful to him.

I'm jealous of him.

It's fucked up.

I unlock her door and offer my hand to help her up. She accepts it with a skeptical look that makes me employ my worst British accent. "Me lady."

"Oh please," she mutters, rolling her eyes.

Chuckling, I head around the back of the Jeep, a bounce in my step. This is the first time we've been alone since she returned for her phone the day of the wreck. No, the second. There was that latte-training incident that I still use for fantasies.

I fire the old Jeep up and glance to her. Her smile is gone. "You doin' okay, Boss?"

She nods. "Just tired."

"I've noticed your work ethic. Hard not to."

She checks to see if I'm teasing. "Are you being a normal person now?"

Backing out of the parking space I give her a smirk. "I don't even know what that means, so I'll say no. I'm not normal."

"No, you're not."

"And you are?"

She wistfully smiles, "No, I guess I'm not either," beautiful eyes drifting away.

Turning left out of the parking lot, Peachtree Street is empty and quiet at this late hour. I look for oncoming traffic as an excuse to linger on her profile. My growing interest has gotten out of hand. I've tried ignoring her, but when you work seven-hour shifts five nights a week with someone you find extremely attractive, it's impossible.

I stand taller when she walks into the main dining room. I do more tricks. I smile more at the clientele. If she comes behind the bar to take care of a computer error or talk about an issue, my skin fires up on the side she's walked by.

I drive her a little crazy, and she's lost her temper with me more than once, but if I don't show her attention she purposefully pulls my focus back to her again. Tonight when Lana and I were laughing about this rich old fart sticking his face in a woman's cleavage right in front of everyone, and getting slapped for it, Meagan called me over and asked me the stupidest question. "Um, do you think we have enough well vodka?"

Surprised, I looked at where we kept the backups, saw they were stocked, and pointed at them, right there in the open. "Yo Boss?"

She blinked a lot and stuttered, "I was just checking to see if you were aware."

"Aware of what?"

"If we had enough."

We stared at each other. A slow smile spread on my face and that made her even more skittish. I leaned in a little and said, "Boo."

She rolled her eyes and rushed away.

I think she's secretly got a thing for me, too.

God I fucking hope so. Otherwise I'm in trouble because she's not forgettable. At least not to me.

Is it because I met her in a crisis? Because I saw her vulnerable and bleeding, is that how this bond cemented in my bones? Carried her to safety when she was hurt, just like so many people—members of my platoon and civilians, even children—I had to carry out of the line of fire when they went down? Is that why I feel like I know Meagan Leigh Forrester more than I do?

All I know is that I haven't been with a woman since I was overseas, and five weeks of watching Meagan's ass wiggle around the dining room has got me hungry for a lot more than just a smile. I want to hear her moan. I want to touch her naked skin. I want to taste her tongue and press inside her until she's clawing into my back with those nails she gnaws on.

I've bruised my cock with how often I stroke it every night just thinking about her. If the thing could talk, it would beg me to stop.

Even my dog rolls his eyes at me now.

The irony to my whacking off all alone is that every single night at Le Marchand phone numbers are discreetly passed to me, often by very beautiful women. Not one has given me the itch I need to scratch. That itch is sitting in my Jeep.

"I need an address, Boss."

"I live near you. Head home. I'll tell you when to turn."

"You know where I live?"

"Of course! Remember I woke up on your couch?"

She glances over and relaxes. "You're messing with me again."

"Nah. Me? I never mess with you."

She gives a half-laugh, half-snort. "Never ever. You never do." Laying her elbow on the door she leans on her hand and stares out the windshield like she's not seeing the view. Something happened between her and Bryan. That's who she's thinking about, which I hate.

"Where'd you go to school?"

"International Culinary School of the Art Institute of Atlanta."

Eyes on the road I mutter, "That's a mouthful."

"It's a very prestigious school."

"As if you'd learn from a small one?"

"There are a lot of good schools that aren't large."

"But *you'd* never go to one of those."

"How do you know that?"

"You're too driven. Anyone who's only twenty-five, yet works eighty-hour weeks without complaint, picks the school that takes them the farthest. You want to succeed so you'd choose only the best."

Appreciative of my assessment, she meets my eyes as I glance to her. "Its lessons had the most subject diversity. And it taught management, Culinary Arts plus Food and Beverage. But now I'm regretting that education." She leans harder on her hand, eyes front.

"Why?"

"Have you seen me making lobster bisque? Have you seen me once wearing a chef coat? Turn right when you get there." She points to the next light. "If I hadn't learned that skill would I be on the floor? Nope."

"Well, you're good at it, if that helps at all."

"It doesn't."

I chuckle and turn the wheel. "Where am I headed?"

"My condo is one street down on the right. I heard you're the last of your brothers to get married."

My eyebrows twitch. "Were you asking about me?"

She glances my way with a look that says no way. "People freely offer up details about you. I guess your family has quite the reputation. But I'd never heard of you."

Can't help but chuckle at her disdainful tone. "This building here?"

"Yes."

I stop alongside a nice Mercedes. The street is full. No open spaces behind us or ahead. Not that it's a good idea to try to invite myself in, but it would take suggesting I park and that's enough time for her to change her mind.

I don't want to stop talking with her, so I turn in my seat and rake a hand through my hair, trying to think of a subject. Meagan meets my eyes.

"Are you posing, Jeremy?"

Dropping my hand I mutter, "Posing? What? No." She cocks her head like she doesn't buy it. "I was thinking."

"Try dandruff shampoo."

"Might be lice."

She laughs, "Gross."

I grin and relax. "Wanna look? I've named 'em."

"You're disgusting."

"Then why have I caught you looking at me so many times?"

Her lips part and her smile falters, then grows. "Because I'm wondering how someone can be so ugly."

"I'm hideous, is that it?"

"Soooooo nasty," she says, caramel eyes glittering in the cutest way. "How do you even walk by mirrors? Do you scare yourself?"

Cracking up I glance away and bite my lip, trying to get serious so I can seduce her. I decide to change the subject, get to know her a little. "You have brothers, Meagan?"

Instantly I regret having asked. From the flash of sadness it's a painful subject.

"I have a sister. We're very close. Used to have a brother…"

My voice deepens. "Your brother died?"

On a quiet nod, she plays with her keys. "Yeah."

"If any of my brothers passed away I'd wanna go with them."

With her head down, she nods again. "I felt that way when I first heard. My mom wouldn't get out of bed for two months. He was her only boy, and the youngest. Her baby." She glances up and sees I'm listening with all the respect this subject deserves, so she quietly continues, "Cecily and I only got out of bed because we had to help Mom."

"Your dad?"

"My poor father disappeared for months. He'd be in the room with us, but he wasn't there, you know?"

"Yeah. My parents would be the same way. I'm so sorry. How did he go? Car accident?"

Meagan pauses. She raises her eyes and confesses, "He killed himself."

My mouth slackens. "I'm sorry," I whisper, meaning it.

She nods, eyes filling up. "Thank you." Breathing in sharply, she shakes her head in an effort to stop the incoming pain. "I'm really tired, Jeremy. Thank you for the ride."

"Of course." Watching her unlock the passenger door, I hurriedly say, "Wait!"

Jumping out I go offer my hand. She slides her delicate fingers onto my palm to step out of the car. But on the sidewalk I draw her into a hug and whisper in her hair, "I'm so sorry about your brother."

I let her go but she doesn't move to leave.

Instead she just stares up at me and comes in for another hug.

I don't question what it means.

She needs a friend.

So I hold her tight and expect nothing.

When she lets me go, I respond in kind, stepping back to give her room to head for home. Leaning against my Jeep I watch her walk away. "I'll wait here and make sure you get in okay. Pop the light on twice when you get inside so I know you're safe."

She smiles over her shoulder. "Okay."

Under the awning of her front door she pauses and waves to me before she disappears. Three seconds later the light flashes twice. The curtains move and I crane my neck a little. She meets my eyes through the window, looking so soft and beautiful. She gives another little wave and disappears.

It's after two in the morning, but she just got me thinking about my own brother, the one I was closest to, who keeps trying to get back in. What have I been doing? What the fuck was I thinking?

I call Jake on the way home and strum my fingers on the steering wheel while I wait for him to answer.

"Jeremy? Everything alright? You okay?"

"Yeah, I'm good. Look, sorry to wake you, but…" I

pause, struggling to say it. "You wanna grab a beer some night this week? Maybe we can go to The Local, like in the old days?"

He pauses and I know he's stunned. His voice is lower as he tells me, "Fuck yes. I'm in." Getting louder and more casual to avoid emotions, he announces, "Bout time you asked me out on a date."

"You're lame."

"No, you're lame."

"I'm hanging up now, Jake."

"I'm going to wait and listen to you breathing."

Cracking up I swipe to hang up the call, muttering, "What a dumbass."

23

MEAGAN

A knock at my door lifts my head up from the magazine. It's nine o'clock on a Sunday, so I'm not expecting anyone. Maybe it's the Jehovah's Witnesses.

Padding to the door in my pajamas I call through the wood, "Who is it?"

"Jeremy!"

My jaw drops and I smooth my hair down, thankful I already brushed my teeth.

What is he doing here?

Swinging it open I find him and his dog on my porch, both panting. "Um…hi, Jeremy. This is shocking."

His deep brown eyes darken and he blinks to the street. "We were taking a run and Aslan dragged me this way. I recognized your street from when I drove you home. Thought I'd see if you're up for a walk since we're neighbors."

My gaze flits down to his intimidating beast. "Oh."

Jeremy reads my reaction and offers, "I was kidding when I said he'd only hurt you if I wanted him to. He's harmless. Pet him." Jeremy roughs up his dog's head and gets a toothy, sloppy-tongued smile as reward. "See? Aslan's just a big goofball."

My heart stops at the name again, but at least this time it doesn't take me by surprise, and I can store memories of Devin away, to be dealt with later. Always later.

"I need to change. Are you in a hurry?"

"Nope."

"Okay...I guess I'll come. Wait here." Closing the door I race to my room and yank on leggings, a long, pink cotton shirt, and my running shoes before I dash into the bathroom to check my hair.

Funny how much I was looking forward to lying around the house and doing nothing until tonight's shift, and then Jeremy shows up and I can't get out of here fast enough.

I've got it pulled into a messy bun atop my head, and it looks casual but good. It would be too obvious if I changed it, right? Probably. A bit of lipstick later and I'm joining them outside.

"That took forever!" Jeremy groans.

I hit his chest and mutter, "No, it did not," forcing myself not to touch his chest again. God, he is so cute.

"I've got grey hair now!"

"You already had grey hair. You're like thirty right?"

"Never ask a guy how old he is," Jeremy smirks, heading to the sidewalk.

"Oh, okay," I mutter with a knowing smirk of my own. "Forty?"

"I'm eighty-seven tomorrow."

Stopping in the path my eyes widen. "Is it your birthday tomorrow?"

He cocks his head. "No, Meagan. I was kidding."

"Well, I knew you were joking about your age but…"

"Come on. We need you to relax, huh, Aslan? Meagan's too literal, isn't she boy?" Jeremy gives a longer lead to his dog, letting him go ahead of us so we can walk together. Our hands are swinging as we walk and I have an insistent urge to hold his. There's an electric current between our fingers like they shouldn't be so separate.

"Why aren't we running?" I glance to him out of the corner of my eye. "Lazy?"

He laughs really loudly. "Yeah! That's me. Hate running. Can't stand it. Never do it. You're on. Aslan, go!" He takes off and I'm just a second behind him.

They pick up speed and I push myself to beat him, but there is no way that's going to happen. I scream as he grabs a leaf and throws it behind him at me.

He laughs and calls back, "That the best ya got, Boss?"

My feet pound the pavement, coming to a loud and sloppy stop. "Okay! We'll walk! Come back."

Chuckling, Jeremy guides Aslan into a U-turn on the sidewalk and returns the twenty or so feet they had on me, while I cross my arms and shake my head. "You should have let me win."

"Yeah, right!" Jeremy scoffs. "And lose your respect. Not worth it."

We match steps and walk up the sunny residential street with birds flitting by above and very few cars passing. "This is nice. I'm glad you came by."

We look at each other and his lips part like he's about to say something. But he changes his mind and faces forward again, his gaze dropping to his beast. "Still scared of him?"

"Not sure yet. Ask me later."

"Okay." We walk in silence for three seconds. "Still scared?"

I grab his bicep, laughing, "Much later!" It's hard to let go, but my fingers finally loosen and drop back to my side.

"I'll take you up on that," he says under his breath.

"Now what's that supposed to mean?"

Jeremy grabs another leaf from a new tree and hands it to me. "This is for you."

"You shouldn't have," I dryly mutter, but I keep it and

ask, "What did you mean before?"

"That I'll ask you later if Aslan scares you," he shrugs.

"No, there was a different tone in your voice. Like you meant something…else."

Jeremy meets my eyes and I stop walking. He pulls on the leash and Aslan sees we're taking a pause, and comes back to sit by us, panting and alert.

Jeremy gazes at me, his voice deepening, the smile gone. "What are you really asking, Meagan?"

It sounded like he meant years later. Like in a future he was planning later. I've caught Jeremy watching me more and more lately at the restaurant. Bryan and I have stopped sleeping together. We fizzled out big time before Jeremy drove me home that night. And this dark-eyed bartender was part of the reason. But I don't know how to tell him that.

Bryan wouldn't stand for us dating. No way would he allow that to go on while he was in charge of us.

"Why are you so serious all of a sudden?" I force a laugh. "I was messing with you. That's what we do, right?"

He eyes me and nods. I step around his dog, giving it a wide berth and Jeremy chuckles. "Yeah, you're still scared."

I'm scared alright. Scared I won't be able to just be friends with Jeremy for much longer. I want to feel his weight on me. I want to see what he tastes like. I want to know how it feels to be pulled into his arms and kissed for hours, even days. I want him, but I want my career more.

24

MEAGAN

Nine whole weeks since the grand opening and I haven't cooked a damn thing here. Haven't prepped a sauce. Haven't marinated a lamb chop. Nothing.

To say I've got one toe out the door would be a lie. Half my body is out.

One of the things that stops me from quitting is how successful it's become. To be associated with this restaurant can only help my career. And we do have fun, the employees and I, with or without Bryan's approval. The time flies by until closing because of the employees, and then I'm reminded all over again as I do the books, that I'm not a fucking general manager so why am I doing this job?

Bryan and I are barely speaking. When it's just us here outside of business hours, fighting in the office, it's hell. I'm not skilled at hiding how I feel. He enjoys treating me with disrespect. That's a lethal mix.

He hasn't come in yet tonight so I'm in a better mood than last night, that's for sure. I threw a chopped carrot at his perfect head. After he'd left the kitchen and couldn't see me do it, of course.

"Where is he?" I mutter while reading the reservation list.

"I haven't had a drink in a whole week," Mira confides in me as the front door opens and a party of six strolls in, all smiles as they glance around and see how packed it is.

"That's great," I whisper, touching her arm. "Keep it up."

"I will." She raises her voice to greet the new guests. "Welcome to Le Marchand. Are there six of you this evening?"

"Seven," one of the men answers as he shakes rain out of his white hair. "My brother is running late."

"Wonderful. What's the name?"

"We don't have a reservation."

Mira glances to me. I hold his eyes and inform him, gently but with authority, "Saturday nights are always busy, but you're welcome to wait in the bar and we can take your name down for the first available."

"How long's the wait?"

Mira glances to her iPad. "An hour, at least."

The group whispers amongst themselves but a woman

in her mid thirties in a Diane Von Furstenberg dress I would kill for, smiles and waves their concerns away. "That's fine! Remember? This is the place from the Bon Appétit article I told you about! With the fancy bartenders! It'll be fun!"

A few faces brighten and their spokesman nods and glances into the restaurant for a look, saying, "Oh, right. Well, good. We'll have some cocktails while we wait." He touches one of his friend's arms. "Give us a chance to catch up."

"And get hammered."

Smiling away from him their spokesman tells Mira, "Name's Conway, thanks."

"We'll let you know the progress, Mr. Conway," Mira smiles. Several of the six are observing her beauty and have to be pulled away from the distraction as the group moves inside.

I take a deep breath and sigh. I cannot wait for tomorrow morning. The only thing I look forward to now is our Sunday walks.

As Mira types his name into the iPad she glances to me. "I heard that. But I don't think they did."

"What? Was I loud? God, I've got to get a hold of myself." I head away and slip a hand in my dress's pocket for my phone. It's vibrating. Again. What an asshole. "Yes, Bryan?"

"I'm not coming in tonight. I got delayed in New Orleans."

I stop, the overflowing and very loud restaurant in front of me as I hush my voice to demand, "You're not even in Georgia right now?"

"No."

"Why didn't you tell me?"

"Since when do I tell you where I am?"

I blink, stunned. "It's Saturday. Our busiest night! Do you need me in the kitchen to cover anyone?"

Like you, the head chef!

What the hell is he doing?

"I called in Pierre. But Meagan, you pull this off on your own tonight, and you just might be cooking tomorrow."

My heart leaps into my throat. "Really?"

"I have to go."

"Okay. Have fun…doing whatever you're doing." He hangs up, and I get the hugest smile on my face. Quick strides bring me to Jeremy's side, behind the bar as he tells a customer, "If you're not happy with him, don't put up with it, Viola."

She looks like he's saying the impossible. "You don't understand, Jeremy! It's not that easy!"

He pours a splash of soda water from the gun over her fresh Chopin Vodka. "Boss needs me. Hold that thought! I'll be right back." He takes me by the elbow and guides me away.

We've become friends since our morning walk, and have even made it a regular Sunday thing, though neither of us planned that aloud. He just showed up the next week, and I happened to be dressed for a walk and waiting by the door, just in case. Same thing happened the following Sunday. And the next.

The conversations have been easy with a lot of teasing and laughter, peppered with tense moments that were dangerously close to making us more than friends.

I know he likes me now, and he must know I'm crazy about him from how happy I am when we're together, and how long I've stretched those morning walks with things like, "Let's just go three more blocks."

"Three, huh? So specific," he chuckled, but didn't tease me more.

We both know without needing to say it, we don't want to get fired. The only safe way to see each other is in daylight where clothes are more likely to stay on.

He's become my confidant with how unhappy I've been with this endless test Bryan has put me through. So naturally I have to tell him my news.

"Why the grin, Boss Lady?" he smiles.

Barely suppressing an excited scream I quietly tell him,

"I'd just begun to give up hope!"

His whole face lights up. "You're going to cook tonight?"

Shaking my head I correct him, and touch his arm. "No, not tonight. But Bryan just told me he's not coming in, that this is my final test and if I pass? I'm cooking *tomorrow* night!"

"He's not coming in tonight?" Jeremy's eyes flicker, then his smile broadens. "You ready?"

I roll my eyes and let go of his arm. He looks down to the empty space where it was, for a quick second.

"I've been ready since before we opened. And I haven't told you this, but on two of my nights off every week I've cooked for my sister Cecily and her husband. All dishes from our menu to stay practiced."

"Well played, Boss." His eyebrows shoot up as his lips purse with appreciation. "Bet they loved that."

"Jealous?"

"Very."

"It's been eating into my salary, but who cares? Cess pitched in, but the ingredients we use are the top of the line, of course. You want to be the best, you have to pay the price!"

We gaze at each other a moment. "True," he says with a look in his eyes that seems to mean more than food cost.

My eyes flash to the ground. "So don't mess up tonight."

He laughs and heads back to his station. "Don't worry, Boss. I've got your back." To Cathy and Lana he calls out, "Hey ladies, what time is it?"

"Wow time!" they both shout.

"And what time is that?"

In unison like a military march song they call back, "Time for a free drink and a free show!"

"What kind o' show?"

"A free WOW show!"

"How do we do it?"

"Right!"

"When do they get it?"

"Right! Now!"

A hush has fallen over the restaurant. Everyone is craning their necks to watch. Some stand. The trio only does this once a night, and word has spread.

One after the other in perfect rhythm they grab a martini glass, slamming the long stemmed base onto rubber drip mats.

First Jeremy. Bam.

Then Cathy. Bam.

Then Lana. Bam.

They all pick them up and slam them twice, at the same time. Bam Bam.

Together they shove their scoopers into the ice and fill the glasses to chill them. Then one after the other like before, they pick up a silver shaker and spin it high in the air, catching and filling it with ice, this time faster than when they got the glasses, but in the same order – Jeremy, Cathy, Lana.

Together they spin vermouth bottles at the same time, catch them upside and pour the clear liquid over the ice in a long stream. Covering the shaker with an upside down pint glass the trio hammers the shakers in the air, in unison, no one out of step, before simultaneously pouring excess Vermouth onto the floor where the drain under the rubber mats will take it away.

Then the order switches. Lana grabs Belvedere vodka and flips it. As she catches it upside down and pours, Cathy grabs Bombay Sapphire gin and flips it. As she pours, Jeremy grabs Grey Goose vodka and flips it, catching and pouring while on the other end, Lana slams her bottle down. She stares ahead like a soldier waiting for the other two to slam their bottles down.

All three shake their martinis and while they do, they grab olives from the condiment trays and toss them to each other. The three flying olives are captured and popped into their mouths instead of the glasses. They chew them, nodding to each other like, *oh, these are so good.*

The room bursts into laughter.

Ice gets dumped, glasses now chilled.

Simultaneously they pour the crystallized martinis into their elegant glasses with each bartender holding the shaker up so high the stream is treacherously long. Without missing a beat they lift the glasses and set them in front of three random guests, saying together, "On the house!"

Applause explodes throughout the restaurant and I am staring at a grinning Jeremy, absolutely thrilled by him. I can't wait for our walk tomorrow morning. I think I'll tell him how amazing that choreographed trick is. They've changed it every week so it's a little different for our regulars. It's such a hit, especially with me.

As the room settles back to normal with people excitedly talking about it Jeremy leans forward to hear a man's order, his thick fingers gripping the bar.

Black button-up shirts look so good on him, with his sleeves tightly rolled up, muscles rippling under the cotton polyester blend. Yummy.

Viola catches me staring at Jeremy's back. She cocks an eyebrow at me, "And they're not bad to look at either."

He turns around for the fridge and meets my guilty eyes. A smile flashes in his, but his lips only smirk like he knows how much I want him. Then he's all focus and I make a hasty exit to do my job. This is us every night at work.

Just friends? Who am I kidding?

The sexual tension crackles between us.

I swear one night I might just lose my reserve and pull him into the women's room to kiss him. Here I am always telling myself that it's all the employees who keep me here.

It's just the one.

Oh fuck it. I don't want to run away like that. Since Bryan isn't here and I have a solitary chance to do this, I stroll purposefully back to the bar and lay my hand on Jeremy's back. He stops making a drink, turns around, his soulful eyes searching mine, "Boss?"

"Thank you for being someone I can confide in."

His lips part and he glances to my mouth. "Of course."

"Jeremy!" Lana calls, swamped.

"I have to go," he smiles, turning around to handle the crowd.

The night goes smoothly. A few small bumps, like running out of vanilla bean sorbet when it's part of our special dessert for the evening. My mistake, I didn't predict how popular it would be. But overall the guests are happy, and employees are, too, since nobody's screaming at them tonight.

In the kitchen after closing Alberto pulls me aside and shakes my hand. "Great job tonight, Meagan."

Gruff beast of a man that he is, he rarely compliments anyone, so I'm ecstatic and shake his hand with equal firmness. "Thank you. You guys were perfect, Alberto. You made it easy for me."

"We've gotta get you back here one day, huh?"

"Maybe tomorrow!"

His eyes flicker with disbelief. "Can't be tomorrow."

I'm immediately defensive as I inform him, "He said if I did well tonight, it was my final test, that I could cook tomorrow night! He said that!"

Alberto makes a face. "Who are you replacing? I've got a full line scheduled for tomorrow night. It's Mother's Day."

My soul crumbles as I stare at Alberto in shock. I totally forgot the holiday what with this big news and me focused on my walk alone with Jeremy and Aslan.

There's no way Bryan would allow my first shift at his precious restaurant to be on the busiest night of the year, a night that's known to be more swamped than even Valentine's Day at dining establishments all across America.

And Bryan knew. He knew and hung the carrot for me to chase after anyway.

"How did I forget it was Mother's Day? I placed the larger order to accommodate it."

With an apologetic look Alberto claps a hand on my shoulder then grabs a grill scraper. He starts cleaning as I walk, dazed, into the office.

25

JEREMY

Outside of the restaurant, Lana and Cathy wave goodbye and climb into their cars. "Goodnight, Jeremy."

"Drive safe," I call after them.

Lana's gold Kia hums to life. Cathy rolls down her window and crooks a finger at me.

I stroll over to her, ear cocked to hear what she has to say. With a hushed voice she asks, "You haven't told Meagan yet, have you?"

"It's not my place."

"No, but it's your *chance*."

"Not that way, Cathy. I'm not a snitch."

"Me neither. But I hate to watch you guys."

"What do you mean?"

"C'mon. It's so obvious how you feel about each other. The only reason Bryan hasn't caught on is because he's so full of himself he'd never believe she chose you." Cathy rolls up the window, puts the car in gear and throws me one last look through the spotless glass that says, *if you don't do something tonight when he's not here, when are you going to?*

Her advice hovers in the air as her red Nissan drives away.

Pacing the lot I ruminate over what she said. When Meagan came back to tell me thank you, it was five deep at the bar, busier than any Saturday we've had, but everyone and everything vanished except for her. When Lana called my name it jarred me back to reality, but for a second there I forgot Meagan and I were supposed to act like we were just friends.

The glowing pink mustache grabs my attention as the Lyft car pulls up in front of Le Marchand.

"Hey!" I call over, making quick strides to his door.

"Sorry, I've got a passenger booked already," he tells me as his window rolls down.

"She cancelled the ride. Here." I pull out a twenty from my wad of tips and hand it to him.

He glances to it, pauses and accepts. It's more than he would've gotten for the one-way fare.

Meagan steps out of the restaurant, sees him and waves.

But I call over to her, "I cancelled the ride. I'll give you a lift. No pun intended."

She blinks in surprise and the driver waits to make sure she's cool with it. He's not rushing away until he's sure because a one-star rating will hurt his livelihood, and all his future bookings. He's probably got a family to take care of.

My heart races while she makes a choice. Feels like everything is riding on this one drop of time. She could get in this guy's car and go home by herself. Or she could let me take her home, and with that choice, the possibilities are endless.

"Well?" the driver asks. "I need an answer."

Meagan stares at me, the breeze blowing her hair as she tells him, "Sorry, you can go."

My pulse quickens and I swallow hard. I would've been devastated if she'd left with him. One more night of not tasting her and I might have gone out of my mind.

He rolls his window up and drives off, leaving a good twelve feet between she and I. Nervously, her eyelashes fall to her bag as she fumbles with the strap. I stride over and take it. "Here. Let me help."

Meagan's eyes meet mine for a charged beat. "I can carry my own purse."

"Which is why your biceps are like a gladiator's."

She melts into laughter. "They are not!"

We head to my Jeep. "They're fucking huge. Are you kidding? I'm as scared of you as you are of Aslan."

She shakes her head as I open the door for her. "I'm not scared of your dog anymore. And my purse isn't that heavy."

"You serious?" I gape at her. "You've got Pluto *and* Jupiter in the thing."

She slides her fingers onto my hand and climbs up, smoothing her dress over her bare knees as she settles in. Taking the offered bag from me she whispers in a conspiratorial tone, "Don't tell NASA."

"Secret's safe with me," I smirk. "All in?"

"Yes."

I shut the door and stroll around the hood, tapping it as I go.

This is my chance.

This is my chance.

This is my fucking chance!

Meeting her eyes through the windshield I tip my head. From the look in her eyes she knows something could happen tonight. She and Bryan haven't been hooking up for well over a month now, my estimated guess. He's dangled the you'll-be-a-chef-soon promise in front of her so long she stopped reaching in the wrong places to get it.

Climbing in, I slide the key in the lock. Even though I look cool on the outside, I'm a fucking mess on the in.

I roll us out of the parking lot and leave the radio off.

The air in here is buzzing loud enough as it is.

"You looking forward to tomorrow night?"

I glance over to see that smile I live for, disappear. "Nope," she quietly says.

"Why? You were great. You even handled Mira sneaking drinks from her flask."

Meagan sighs and rests her elbow on the door, leaning on it. "Poor girl. She's got a problem. So of course she keeps lying and saying she's better."

The streetlamps of Buckhead hauntingly trace Meagan's profile like a heartbeat of golden light. Suddenly I remember her wrapped in a blood-soaked airbag. What if she'd died that day? I blink back to the road.

"Jeremy, the thing is, it's Mother's Day tomorrow. It's the busiest restaurant night of the year."

"So? You can do it! I'll be there cheering you on!" She glances to me and I meet her eyes to add, "I'll pop into the kitchen and give you a thumbs up every ten minutes, even if Lana yells at me like she did tonight."

Meagan softly laughs and looks out her window. "I wish."

"If I say I'll do it, I will."

From a thousand miles away she whispers, "Bryan will never let my first night be on a holiday. He must have forgotten."

Anger explodes in my core.

What a fucking dick.

He didn't forget shit!

He's the most manipulative and calculating bastard I've ever met in my life. He plays us all and because it's his restaurant, he gets away with it. If this job hadn't changed my life I'd fuckin' clock him 'til his face never looked the same. See how well his ego could handle a hit like that, the conceited sonofabitch would wilt and whine like the pussy he really is without his pretty looks.

Bullies are fucking cowards on the inside.

"You look like you're going to punch the windshield, Jeremy."

I glance over with fire in my eyes. "Not what I want to hit."

"Bryan."

"Yeah."

"Me too," she sighs, leaning onto her hand and staring at the road. Rain starts spattering the windshield, which surprises neither of us. Raindrops are as synonymous with Georgia as peaches are.

I reach for her hand, the one resting on her thigh, and clasp it. "I'm sorry, Boss."

She squeezes back. When I go to bring my hand back, she tightens her hold. Well, okay then.

"Stay," she tells me in a soft voice.

I just nod and drive.

Our fingers start to move, twining together then unlacing and tracing the lines before we twine them again. My breath shortens, my cock wide-awake. I don't know what to do with myself. First time I've touched a woman like this in maybe two years. I'm not counting the espresso machine incident. That was me trying to get a rise out of her for the fun of it, only. My heart wasn't in it. And I'm not counting the hug because that was as a friend, and a person who loves his family and could imagine the pain of losing one.

This is intimate. It has consequences. And right now I'm willing to pay them.

Her skin feels so warm. Our fingers lace and tighten in a firm grasp that feels like there's a decision behind it. And a future.

"Turn right at the light."

"I remember."

I stop in front of her condo, give her hand a quick squeeze before I let go and jump out. Running in the thickening downpour my hair mats to my head. I open her door and help her down. With her purse in both hands she gazes up at me like she wants to say something.

"I'm *not* leaving, Meagan. I'm letting you out so you won't walk in the rain. I'll park the car and come back."

"But what about…"

"I don't care what Bryan thinks anymore."

"He'll fire both of us if he finds out."

"I don't fucking care."

"Yes, you do." She tilts her head as the rain pelts it.

Wiping my face I confess with the agony of a decision. "You're right. I do. I care a lot. But Boss? You listenin'?" She nods, frowning deeply. "I can't go another night not knowing what you taste like."

"Wow," she whispers.

"If I'm about to lose my job I want to do it smiling."

She laughs, "You're insane!"

"Maybe. Probably. I'm going to park that Jeep and come running back to you. Don't turn me away. Don't stop this from happening."

Her eyes warm up and she whispers, "I'll wait for you."

"Wait for me inside." I touch her hair. "This storm is only going to get worse."

To hide my obscene bulge I shove my hands in my pockets and stroll quick as I can to get in the Jeep. I'm fucking elated this is actually happening. There's a space on the street just up ahead. I saw it. Spotted that thing like a hawk scanning a field for its dinner. I make use of it as quickly as possible, jamming the gear into park so hard I could rip the gearshift off.

I don't want her changing her mind before I get back.

I hit the wet street running, only slowing when I find her waiting right where I left her. "You're drenched! I told you to wait inside!" When she makes no move to explain I stand in front of her, both of us beaten up by the downpour as we stare at each other.

"The rain's hiding my tears."

"Oh, fuck, Meagan. I'm so sorry."

Her face squishes with pain. "I want to be a chef! I need to see people enjoying what I've made! I need it. Why is he doing this to me?"

I pull her into my arms, water encapsulating us. Her shoulders shake as she holds me close, face tucked into my chest.

"Shhh, it's gonna be okay. It's just making you stronger for when you have your own restaurant. Your own guests. Your own rules. Your own menu."

She looks up at me. "I want that! When am I going to have my turn?"

"Whenever you want it," I huskily tell her.

Being this close to her after harboring a blistering crush has me fired up in every way. Her long, raindrop covered eyelashes fall toward my lips as hers part. I don't hesitate or second-guess. I crush her mouth to mine in the kiss I've been dreaming about. Her hands slide up my back as I tighten my grip on hers. I unlock her mouth with my own and seek out her tongue for the first time. God, how I've waited for this. She feels better than I thought she would. The kiss isn't awkward or tentative, it's hungry and desperate for more. We've both waited for this. I lead the way, and she moves with me.

Suddenly I'm lifting her up and hooking her legs around my hips while I hold her on me. She gasps and separates a quick heartbeat to look into my eyes, then collapses into a new kiss, her lips so perfect and yielding that I groan and tear away from them to tell her, "I want you so badly. God, every Sunday we've spent together it's been fucking heaven and it's been fucking hell."

She grins, "For me too!"

We kiss like two people starved for one another. I break away and pant, "Are you ready for this? Because I won't want just one night."

"Oh my God," she murmurs as rain splashes her parted lips.

Looking around her shoulder to see where I'm going, I carry her to her door. She tucks her head into my neck and kisses it, the purse smacking against my ass along the way.

"Your tank's gonna leave a mark," I joke in her ear as the rain gets louder.

She cracks up, "Sorry!"

"Let it swing. I'm enjoying the beating. It's making me realize this isn't a dream."

The sight of her with her lipstick smudged, smiling and drenched, downpour attacking us and we don't even care, it stills me deep in my soul. My smile fades, and hers goes away with it. I close my eyes as she cups my cheek, and open them again to say, "I've waited for this."

She blinks and frowns, "I have to get my key out."

"Wait." I carry her to a dry place under her awning, set her down and as she searches, I wipe my face with both hands, feeling like she just disappeared from me a little. "Was that too much, what I just said?"

She holds my look and shakes her head. "No. It wasn't too much. I've waited for it, too." She turns around and leads the way in.

26

MEAGAN

I feel suddenly nervous. Something bigger than I'd imagined is happening to Jeremy and I.

Inside, he is on me in an instant, cupping my face in his hands and kissing me. All of my anxiety is replaced with happiness. I'm smiling like crazy as he kisses my chin, my nose, my closed eyelids. We start to peel each other's wet clothes off, our fingers sliding sensually over every exposed inch of slippery wet skin. We kick off our shoes, kiss, then look down to watch our fingertips tracing naked shoulders, rib cages, belly buttons. I can't stop touching his gorgeous chest. He slips his soaked fingers under my bra straps and slides the right one down, then the left, and kisses me before taking it all the way off. I've never been undressed like this before, like I'm a gift he's relishing.

He leans over and tugs off my wet socks, then his own as I stare at his back rippling. As he kisses my knees once each, I trace his spine and he shivers and rises up to pull me to him again, kissing me like I'm being kissed the right way for the first time. I'm in my panties and he's in his boxers, which are plastered to our goosebump-covered skin.

I reach up, lace my fingers into his hair as he bends and kisses my painfully taut nipples. Jeremy cups my breasts, heating them up with his lips, one at a time and so tenderly. His hands slip around my naked sides and he presses in and brings me closer. He molds our lips hungrily seeking out my tongue.

I'm the one being kissed like this.

It's my back his strong fingers are pressed into like he won't let me go.

It's my name he's murmuring, like he wants only me.

I pull away from our kiss and search his soulful brown eyes. There are little specks of gold in them and I get lost with my questions as he gazes back at me without trying to hide.

"What are you thinking?" Jeremy asks me, his voice deeper.

I whisper, "I guess I'm a little scared, Jeremy."

He kisses my nose. "Of?"

"Of how much I want this."

"Where's your bedroom?"

"Hallway, first door on the left."

My breath hitches as the fingers of his right hand slide under my ass dangerously close to my crack as he carries me while we kiss. He lets go to glance over my shoulder and not run into anything. I bite his neck. He groans and walks faster. "Fuck I haven't been this hard in…" He doesn't finish, but I want to know the rest.

"In how long?"

In the hallway he meets my eyes. "Years." He kicks the door on the left open and starts to take me in, but stops. "This is the bathroom."

I laugh, "Gotcha!"

He chuckles and carries me into my bedroom—on the right—tossing me onto the bed. "Nice one, Boss."

"Oh my God, keep calling me that," I smile, teasing him.

"You like to have the power, Meagan?"

I nod, biting my lips on a grin. "Maybe."

He smirks like he never had any doubt. Holy crap, Jeremy Cocker standing at the edge of my bed, is staring down at me with lust in his eyes. I've touched myself to this fantasy, and now it's really happening. He's really here.

"I fucking love your breasts," he groans, his gaze massaging them.

"Not too small?"

He makes a noise like I'm crazy. "They're yours, so

they're perfect. You want to see something that's small?" He slides his wet boxers down his thighs and his enormous cock bounces out. "Tiny, huh?" he grins.

Covering my face with my hands I start laughing again. "Yes, itty bitty. What am I going to do with it?" I throw my hands down and say, "Seriously! What am I going to do with that monster?!"

He laughs, palming himself for a quick beat before he dives onto me, sliding up my naked flesh until his lips devour mine. My legs have opened instinctually and I moan as his cock begins to grind, lengthwise, against the wet crotch of my panties. Only the silky fabric is between us and I claw his back, my pussy pulsing so hard.

He hisses through his teeth with pleasure as we grind, and my moans grow faster and higher. "Fuck this," he growls.

"Fuck me!"

He locks eyes with me, slides his tongue urgently in my mouth then drops down and inches my panties off, gazing at my pussy for the first time. I'm watching him stare like he hasn't seen a naked woman ever. My throbbing pussy is aching for his touch and when his face disappears between my legs I cry out. He licks me like he loves it. Like every slip of the tongue is a turn-on to him. His tongue strokes my clit in long, soft up and down strokes, then dips into a side of it and flicks, then pauses, his hot breath driving me insane. I moan as he keeps teasing me, flicking again, stopping again, then more tiny flicks, each round slightly longer than the last. The tension builds as my walls open to receive him, my folds swelling with need. "I'm going to cum," I moan.

"I know," he murmurs against my flesh, pushing my legs open wider where he slides his tongue just once up my slit then slides a finger in and starts to slowly pump while tonguing me until I lose my mind.

"Oh Jeremy," I moan as heat spreads out. "Jeremy!" The orgasm begins and as the waves threaten to crash he rises up, positions his cock against my shivering opening to fill me with the slowest possible thrust, while I'm climaxing. It's exactly what I need in this moment. I break open to him as my pussy clenches his huge cock with hot bursts of pleasure. I scream as he drives it all the way in and groans into my mouth.

He starts fucking me slowly, his arms slipping under my back. We're gripped together as we fuck, our mouths endlessly kissing, interrupted only by sensual moans. He's so hard and big I am constantly brought to the edge and kept there. He breaks free of our kiss and searches my eyes, panting. "Hey," he whispers, smiling.

"Hi," I softly laugh. We gaze at each other a moment and then he takes my mouth and unlocks my jaw with his, increasing the pressure everywhere before he releases me and bites my neck.

"Oh God," I moan, my head falling back as his cock and his bite render me boneless. "I'm cumming. Cum with me, Jeremy," I whisper. He nods once and crushes me in a kiss, groaning into my lips as my walls quake around his length.

His shaft thickens, filling up. He shouts, "Holy fuck!" exploding inside me, his muscular arms squeezing me so hard as he loses control. I'm throbbing in time with my heartbeat, clenching around his cock. I cry out and he crumbles into my neck, gnawing on it. "Boss, I'm still cumming. Can't stop. Fuck, this was pent up for you for so fucking long."

"I know," I whimper. "I love it."

He's panting. So am I. He meets my eyes as the aftershocks hit. He shakes his head. "I'm fucking crazy about you, Meagan. I haven't been able to stop thinking about you."

My breath hitches and I lace my fingers into his hair to whisper, "You're scaring me."

"You'll learn to trust me."

Blinking at him I mutter, "Jeez, your confidence is amazing."

A grin flashes, but he tones it down to a sexy smirk and says, "Let's just see how this goes."

"Oh, right, you guys only spend one night with the

women you sleep with."

He cocks an eyebrow, the smirk unfazed. "What are you talking about?"

"Lana told me. You're a wham-bam-thank-you-ma'am bunch."

With confusion darkening his eyes, he asks, "Who is? Who are you talking about?"

"All of the Cocker Brothers."

Jeremy blinks at me, then bursts out laughing. "Is that the town gossip about us?"

"Yes!"

He keeps laughing, practically crying it's so funny to him. "Oh shit, that's good."

"Is it true?"

"Yeah. Totally one hundred percent true."

I stare at him, appalled. But then his eyes sparkle in that mischievous way I'm so used to now. "You're messing with me again."

"One." He kisses my lips. "I already told you out there in the rain that I want this to be more than one night. And two." He kisses me again. "I'm still inside you. What kind of an asshole would I be to tell you something like that and still be buried in you?"

"A big one."

"Exactly." He chuckles and holds my eyes, growing

serious. "Lana isn't someone you can trust, Meagan. Let's just leave it at that."

"And you are?"

"Fuck yes." He kisses my nose.

"Are you getting hard again?"

Jeremy answers by fucking me senseless two more times.

27

JEREMY

It's almost four in the morning. I could go another round. Hell, I could keep going into Sunday afternoon, but I have a dog at home waiting to relieve himself. Can't ignore that responsibility.

Pulling the covers over Meagan's limp and naked body, I smile into her sleepy eyes. "I've gotta walk Aslan. He's probably bursting at the seams right about now."

Her delicate hand floats up to my jaw. "Can you come back afterward? Bring him over here."

I nod. Meagan sure does keep me guessing. "Sure. He's never slept anywhere but home before, but he's a laid back buddy. He'll love it."

She smiles and buries herself under the covers. "It's cold without you."

"I'll be back in a flash."

"Take my keys and lock up, then let yourself back in."

"Whatever you say, Boss."

She chuckles and peeks out at me as I back out of the room, cock swinging. I give her a last little wave, then rush back in and jump, landing on top of the covers and kissing her. She's laughing but kisses me back, slipping her arms around my neck and moaning into my lips.

"Fuck, I'm getting hard again." I do a push-up over her body, then push down, kiss her and jump up to standing. "I'll be back."

"Hurry!"

Heading out I wince at the notion of putting on wet clothes again. Shit is going to be cold! As my bare feet slap the hardwood floor I glance around her cozy home and see inside her mind a bit. She's got style and cares about how her place looks. Someone could photograph this for a magazine, she's done it up so well.

Wincing, I tug on my dripping, black slacks, leave my work shirt open a second while I adjust to the cold. Bending over I forgo the socks, shoving my dry feet into wet work shoes. It's a battle getting them in so my head turns as I grunt. My eyes land on a framed photograph sitting on her little table here, and I snatch up the frame and stare at it. My heart stops.

"Devin," I groan, hurting so bad as all those memories from my nightmares slam into me. "Oh, fuck," I croak,

"Devin!"

"Jeremy?"

I whip around, the photograph in my hand. Meagan is in the doorway in a white terry cloth robe, frowning at me. Tears are rushing down my face and I can't stop them. Barely able to talk I choke out, "You're his sister?"

She nods, face twisting with confusion as she walks to me. "You knew Devin?"

My eyes drop back to the photograph, my best friend in the Marines staring back at me, his smile frozen from where he kneels on the sand, his hand on his German Shepherd's neck. "That's why the name Aslan upset you. It was Devin's dog. You knew its name."

"Jeremy, what's going on? How do you know them?"

From a far away place the story tumbles out of me like it's been waiting for the moment when I faced my biggest ghost. "Aslan saved us. Barked for us to get back. The warning we'd heard so many times. But he'd gotten too close. He detonated a trigger. Devin screamed. I'll never forget the pain in his scream as he watched his best friend get blown to bits before our very eyes. Little pieces landing everywhere. On us."

"Oh my God, you were in his platoon," she whispers, tears streaming down her face now as she covers her mouth with her hands.

"It wasn't the first time Aslan saved us. All the other days he sniffed 'em out, no problem, before they were triggered. Devin wasn't just his handler, he planned on keeping him when his time was served. They were closer than any team of dog and man I'd seen in my four years as a Marine."

Meagan moans in pain, "I can't believe you knew my brother?"

"Knew him? He was my best fucking friend." I lock eyes with her, my face twisted up. "But when Aslan died, Devin disappeared right with him."

"Oh Jeremy, please tell me a story about him. We have no idea who he was out there. Please tell me." She falls into my arms.

Kissing her hair I rasp, "Lemme think. God it hurts to remember. Devin laughed at stupid shit. He made me forget where we were. All of us felt like that about him. When we tracked Isis, he joked, 'Of course they had to name their crazy after a woman!'" Meagan makes a face like she's fake upset, but laughs through her tears, because she can see him fucking around like that. "He and that dog, they were like our mascots. He joked around, and Aslan was his constant shadow, letting us love on him whenever we were feeling depressed or freaked or just plain lonely for our families. Which was a lot of the fuckin' time. You get hardened to it.

But not Devin. He wouldn't let that happen. That dog helped him stay *him*."

Meagan's listening like she just got a miracle, a chance to spend time with him again, just by listening. "Tell me more," she whispers. "Oh, you must be freezing."

"What?" I glance down to the wet clothes. "I don't care," I croak, gazing at her. "God, Meagan, you're his sister? How did I not see that?"

"Did he talk about me?"

"Fuck yes! He always talked about his sisters, and how beautiful they were, and how we weren't allowed to touch them," I grin through the tears. "But he never said your names. We used to give him such shit and he said, 'Hell no! If I ever get out of this hell and you fuckers come with me, hands off my sisters. Ya hear me? I'm not telling you anythin' else about 'em!' God, we used to say we'd fight over them...over you! Holy fuckin' hell. I can't believe you're Devin's sister." I gaze at her, stunned by the synchronicity that brought us together. "He'd kick my ass if he knew I was here."

Meagan smiles through her tears, too. "I wish he had that chance. I think he could've taken you"

"Ha! Never. But I'd love to see him try."

She rises on her toes and kisses me. "Let's go walk *your* Aslan, together. We can talk more on the way. I want to hear

213

every story you have."

"Go get dressed."

She nods and clasps my hands before heading back. My eyes drop to the photograph and I shake my head under the pain, not only of my loss but of hers. "You fuckin' asshole," I whisper to his smiling face. "Why'd you have to do it?"

Meagan calls out to me that she has something dry for me to wear.

I glance to the hallway and see her walking toward me in jeans and t-shirt, holding a blue sweater out. "This was his. I gave it to him before he deployed, so I kept it after he... You can borrow it."

I groan, "Oh shit," taking it from her. "It's an honor. Thank you." I hastily strip and slide Devin's sweater over my head.

It fits like a favorite glove.

Meagan puts on a fresh pair of boots, and a warm coat she had on a hook by the front door, grabs her keys, glances to the sweater with memories in her eyes before she turns around and we head out.

28

MEAGAN

Jeremy extends his hand to help me down from the Jeep. "There's a puddle so watch out."

"Thank you." His grip tightens and I use his guidance to leap to a dry patch. The rain stopped while we were in my bed, but it's left behind small lakes as far as the eye can see.

"So we were bathing in buckets, with water the guys before us used. It was nasty, but Devin used it as an excuse to lighten our moods. He streaked naked around the camp shouting, 'If anyone else needs a shower I'll pee on you! It'll be cleaner I promise!'" Jeremy and I crack up laughing as we stop on his small front porch. Through his grin he continues, "Best part was that one of our guys was gay. We all knew it and didn't care, especially because he made up for his secret by being a bigger badass than most of us, like he had something to prove. Still, we liked to fuck with him. All in fun. That's what you do in the Marines. No one is safe. We swear, smoke, and try and get a rise out of each other. So Devin stopped running, pointed at Larry and shouted with a shit-eating grin, 'Except you, Larry! You'd enjoy it waaaaaaay to much!' Then he took off running. God, it was so funny! Larry turned bright red and huffed off. Oh my God, the rest of us were dyin'!"

He slides the key in the lock while I ask, "Where was Aslan?"

"Running with him!" Jeremy grins, but then he loses the levity and sadness jumps back on him. He blinks it away and mutters, "They were inseparable."

Swinging the door open, his huge dog is waiting and runs outside so excited that he's kind of half leaping, too big to jump really high. Jeremy kneels and pets him. "Sorry, boy. Didn't mean to leave you hanging. A woman got in the way of my duties."

"Hey!" I cry out.

Jeremy chuckles and sends his Aslan out to the yard. "It's too wet for a walk, so I'll just let him roam out here. You want to wait inside while I watch him? Keep warm?"

Shaking my head a little, I step closer to Jeremy and burrow into him. "No, I want to be here."

He embraces me and tightens his hold, kissing the top of my head. "This is where I want you."

Turning my head so my cheek is tucked against his

collarbone, I watch his dog roam the small yard as if it's the first time he's smelled it – everything is interesting all over again. "So he didn't get his name from the book?"

"Nah," he whispers in my hair.

"You didn't want a Shepherd?"

"I didn't pick his breed. He was a gift."

"Who gave him to you?"

"Some kids dropped him out of their car because they didn't want to take care of him. He landed right over there, in front of my house."

Shocked, I lock eyes with Jeremy. "Who would do that to a puppy?!!"

"Idiots," he mutters. "Some people don't understand responsibility. I think Israel's got it right on that front."

"What do you mean?" Now I understand why Jeremy's eyes have so much depth. After all the things he's seen, there's a shadow of knowledge of the darker side of life. "What are they doing in Israel?"

"At eighteen everyone has to do two years of service in their armed forces. Has to. Even the women. Boot camp teaches you discipline. You grow up. No whining. No running from responsibility. You learn loyalty to others and to your home. To your country. We were like a family. And better than most of the ones we'd left behind."

"We had a good family!" I object, instantly defensive.

I even start to pull away but Jeremy quickly says, "Hey hey, no. Stop. Not yours. Devin had no complaints. I promise I would tell you, but he had none, I swear. I meant other guys who enlisted to get away from abuse. Or neglect. Aslan, come!" Jeremy whistles and his dog comes bounding through the darkness, the whites of his eyes and his teeth visible first.

As wet paws slap by us into the house I say, "Look at his smile."

"Yeah, he needed that. Come inside, beautiful." Jeremy guides me in and shuts the door. He adjusts the thermostat and soon we can hear the heater switch on, a quiet whir from the vents. "I'm going to change into some dry pants and shoes."

I sit down on the couch I'd woken up on. Haven't been back here since that day. So much has changed since then. Except this house.

Everything is the same as it was. I rise up and quietly walk to the kitchen to see if there's evidence of a life there. But the counters are bare save for a clean spatula on a black towel. I so want to check the refrigerator. It's starting to make sense why he lives this way.

I was so wrong about him.

Crossing through the living room I knock on his bedroom door. Aslan barks from inside and Jeremy quiets him before opening the door and pointing at me. "Can't you see it's still her? What, are you that not used to having someone else here that you forgot already?"

He's in Devin's sweater, blue jeans, and dry socks, looking exactly like the person who would have been my brother's friend. He sees my reaction and his smile vanishes.

"You want me to take this off? If it's too hard to see me in it—"

"No, it's just that...Jeremy, do you live like this because of your time in the Marines?"

A quick frown pierces his distinct brow line and he walks to the bed and starts making it, the way people busy their hands when they're uncomfortable. "I don't know. Hadn't thought about it. What's wrong with my place?"

Suddenly the zipper on my coat has become very interesting as I play with it and mutter, "Nothing. It's a nice home."

Aslan ambles over to me and nudges my fingers. I give him a tentative pet. He might weigh the same as me, he's that huge. But then he turns his body in a right U-turn and presses his weight into me. It's extremely adorable so I bend to pet him with more enthusiasm. "Good boy," I whisper. He lobs his head up, tongue hanging out as I scratch behind his ears. "You like that?" I smile, growing more comfortable.

"The breed is good with women and kids. Protective."

From under my eyelashes I glance to Jeremy. "Oh?"

"Because they're powerful and scary-looking some people breed only the most aggressive ones or the largest. But they're usually like what you see here. My brother's daughter, they love each other. Aslan helped her through a hard time." Jeremy walks to me, takes my hand and pulls me to him, softly kissing my lips before he admits, "I haven't decorated much."

"Your place is great!"

A grin flashes. God, I want to kiss him all the time. "Liar. But it's *my* place, Boss Lady, and I get to live how I want."

"I know. Of course you do. What if I told you to get a throw blanket and some pillows for the couch?"

"I'd tell you to mind your own business," he huskily replies.

Smiling and growing more attracted by the second, I ask, "How about if I said that you need some art. At least one picture."

He kisses my nose and cocks an eyebrow. "I'd say, Meagan, you better like me the way I am or don't like me at all."

"You're so fucking sexy," I murmur against his lips before I rise up on my toes to kiss him like I mean it.

Our tongues taste each other and he groans into me as

I press my body against him.

"You have eggs at your place?"

I have eggs in my body that wake up around you.

Smiling at my hormones I nod, "I do have eggs. Cage free."

"Ooooh, special eggs."

"You have no idea," I murmur. "But I'm not cooking them for you."

"Thought you want to be a chef."

"If I have the eggs, you cook the eggs. I'm not supplying the food and cooking it, too. Sorry, buddy. I'm not your mommy."

Jeremy laughs, "No shit. My mother is far nicer than you are. Fair enough." He glances to Aslan. "Hey buddy, you want to sleep over at a beautiful woman's house? She won't make you breakfast but she will pet you." Jeremy kisses my fingertips. "Let me get my boots on."

Crossing to the bed I sit down and notice his practically empty closet. The man has no clothes to speak of, just the bare minimum of everything, and I don't care what he says, I now know why. When they were out there, his platoon had to be ready to move at a moment's notice. I remember Devin writing and telling me that.

Suddenly I gasp, "Oh my God!"

He glances over. "What'd you just remember?"

"The show behind the bar! That's inspired by the drills, isn't it? I can't believe I've watched you all those times and didn't realize you were a Marine."

A sneaky smile tugs at him. "The bottles are my rifle. And the girls don't know it, but they've been through their own sort of infantry training." He chuckles and slams his boots on the floor like he's kicking them into shape. "Only theirs was a lot more fun."

"I can't believe I didn't see it before."

"If you'd gone through boot camp, you wouldn't have missed it. Come here." Jeremy extends his hand and I walk to him, sliding my fingers over his. Both of us watch, feeling the warmth of our skin touching and the pulse of life that runs through us.

I slip my arms around his neck, caressing it. His body is made of marble with a thin layer of smooth, soft skin over it. His kiss is filled with emotion and I instinctively know that he's thinking of my brother, and how strange it is that I'm in his arms.

"Before we go any further, Meagan…" he trails off, searching my eyes.

"Further than having sex three times?" I tease him. "Further than my being in your bedroom at five in the morning? Further than you wearing…this?"

"I'm serious, Meagan. No joking right now."

My smile fades. "Okay."

"Before we get anymore involved, I have to tell you something so it doesn't come up later."

Frowning I gaze up at him. "What?"

"I was the one who found him. It was me."

Agony clouds my vision as hot tears jump up.

Jeremy swallows hard. "It was two days after Aslan died. The platoon got called to check something out after rumors of…anyway, he needed his rifle. I told him he should sit this one out. That he wasn't ready. The look in his eyes was so determined. He told me, 'I have to do it.' I thought he meant he had to fight with us. He had to take the men down who'd set those bombs where Aslan found them. I was all for it. Thought it was healthy. Would help him grieve to find justice. But then he went back into his tent alone. Nothing abnormal in that, so I didn't stop him. Then I heard the shot." Jeremy clears his throat. "I ran in. I started shouting, praying, yelling at God, begging for time to go backwards. The guys in our platoon came running. They pulled me away. I fought them. Punched a couple. Devin was my best friend out there. I didn't want to leave him. So I stayed."

"Oh my God," I whisper.

"I just, I needed to tell you, since you'd shared with me that one night I drove you home that he killed himself. When I realized tonight that you were talking about Devin, I had to tell you it was me who found him. I didn't want that secret between us."

"I understand. Oh my God, that must have been so awful."

His face twists in agony as he pulls away from me and shakes his head. "Still haunts me. See him all the time."

"You don't blame yourself."

"No, course not. Come on, boy. Time to go." Aslan runs into the living room. Jeremy waits for me to walk out first.

But I stop in front of him and lay my hands firmly on his chest. "Of course you do. I do! I blame myself. Cecily blames herself. Mom and Dad, they both think they weren't good enough parents!" Jeremy's frown deepens as he takes in what I'm saying. "Of course you blame yourself, just like we do. You can't help it when someone you love decides to go, and leaves you here all alone. But we're wrong. Because we can't control what other people do, ever. If you had stopped him, he would've found another way."

"You don't know that."

"I know Devin. And when he set his mind on something, nobody could stop him! He was so stubborn!"

Jeremy breaks into low laugh of recognition, a pain-filled chuckle that begs to be relieved of the ghost he's been carrying. "He was a stubborn bastard."

Smiling and ripped wide open, I nod and whisper while resting my hand on Jeremy's heart. "It's not your fault. *I* don't blame you. Look at me. I don't blame you for what my brother did. I will never blame you for that."

Jeremy clears his throat and covers my hand with his. He brings my fingers to his lips and presses them there, closing his eyes. "I loved him."

I burrow into Devin's sweater and whisper, "Me too."

29

MEAGAN

It's a handful of quiet minutes before we're back in my home and I'm filling a glass bowl with water while Jeremy hangs the leash on my coat hooks.

"Jeremy?"

"Yeah?" He leans against the doorframe in my kitchen, hands shoved in his pockets.

"Can I tell Cecily the stories you shared with me tonight?"

He pushes off the doorframe and walks to me. "Of course. Your parents, too."

"Okay, I'm going to tell you something."

He gives me a lopsided smile while scratching Aslan's ears. "You're nervous, so it's probably about how much you like me."

"Maybe I like you," I whisper before he gives me a soft kiss.

"Maybe?"

"Yes, that's all you're getting out of me."

Jeremy laughs and lifts me up, carrying me into my bedroom and setting me down. As he starts to undress me, his voice is low. "I'm tired and feel a little beat up. I'm going to hold you and just sleep. But I want you naked."

"I'd love that. My face is swollen from the crying. I'd love to cuddle."

"I'm a fantastic cuddler."

"Oh?" I ask with a cocked eyebrow.

"I think. I can't remember, it's been so long."

The best part about that is he wasn't teasing or joking that time. He means it, and I wish it were the same for me. I wish I had never slept with Bryan. Being with Jeremy makes it seem ridiculous. That man, in every way, gave me crumbs. So embarrassing.

I slip under the covers to stay warm and watch Jeremy undress. "Your chest is gorgeous," I whisper.

"Not as hot as yours."

"Not one woman. All those phone numbers I've seen them give you." His eyebrows shoot up. "Yes! I've been watching. I saw! I'm the first woman you've been with since opening night?"

"You're the first in two years." Jeremy slides his pants down.

My lips part on sight of him. "You're hard."

"This? This is half-mast." He palms it and closes his eyes. My stomach clenches as I watch him. He meets my look, his darkened with need now. "Okay, might have to do something about this."

"We can't let it go to waste," I smile.

A grin flashes as he climbs onto the bed, naked on all fours. "Maybe we just do it nice and slow."

Jeremy pulls back the covers and runs his fingers down my sides, kissing me. He flips us over so that I'm on top of him and I hover above his erection, the crimson shaft pulsing, veiny and gorgeous. Just looking at it, I want him more by the second. I slide down onto his length, breathing sharply inward as it penetrates me. Jeremy's watching, his hands on my hips then traveling down legs. He reaches up and rubs the pad of his thumb over one of my hard nipples.

We both moan as my pussy yields and become wetter. As he nestles up against my cervix, our backs arch and we lock eyes, eyelids heavy. Our bodies start to move of their own volition and we let them lead the way. I bend to kiss him as we fuck, and our tongues taste each other in between panting breaths and deep, long moans.

Jeremy sits up and slides his arms around me, flipping me over and holding up one of my legs as he grinds into me with a steady thrusting rhythm. "So wet, baby," he groans, his head falling back as he closes his eyes.

"Oh God," I moan, digging my fingers into his muscles, sliding my short nails down his sexy V. He dives into me, stretching and filling me, sometimes leaning down to take my mouth in his. It's long and slow and sensual. His kisses never hurry. They draw out the pleasure from my core. Heat drifts from my center and tingles spread into my limbs. I begin to lose control. Jeremy's breath blending with mine, the deep-throated grunts he's making, I love it all. I love to hear how much this turns him on. I love to hear the sounds. I love the way he smells. I moan loudly and crane my hips up. His cock is perfect, hard and smooth and slippery. He shivers, bends down and bites my chin, kissing down my neck and taking my earlobe between his teeth. I moan and press my breasts into his muscles as the contractions start.

"Boss, I can feel you clenching. God, you're so fucking wet." We crash together in a kiss, our hips pounding and grinding, our thighs tangled and everything on fire. Jeremy roars, "Fuck yeah!" and fills me with his hot, sticky semen while I bury my face in his neck, whimpering.

When we're wrapped around each other and I finally begin to drift off, I hear Jeremy groggily mumble, "I probably could use a nice blanket like this."

My heart melts a little with that admission. He was so defensive when I suggested that his living in such a barren home might be because of what he'd been through. Maybe from survivor's guilt he thought he didn't deserve comfort.

I trace his shoulder and kiss it. "Aslan's sleeping. He seems to like it here."

With his eyes closed, Jeremy's mouth turns up a little. "He's not alone."

I snuggle into him, whisper, "Neither are you," and fall asleep smiling.

30

JEREMY

Her phone ringing wakes me up around ten o'clock. Meagan's arm is wrapped over my chest, and she doesn't budge at first. The second ring rouses her and she blinks awake, lifting her head to mumble, "Is that mine?"

"Yeah."

She groans and rolls off of me, petting Aslan's head as he groggily stands up for the attention. I watch her naked ass tick back and forth. "You're beautiful!" I call after her.

She laughs to herself, but then I hear her sigh. That impatient little sound alerts me to who's calling. I hadn't thought about the fact that it might be him.

My mind was busy. Last night was the first time I didn't have the dream about finding Devin. I don't remember any of my dreams from last night, and that hasn't happened in years.

"Hello?" I hear her answer from the living room.

"What time is it?" After a pause, she says, "Well, I'm sorry. I slept in!" Another pause. "I know what day it is. It's Mother's Day, which means you weren't going to let me cook tonight, were you?"

Naked, too, I walk out there feeling protective of her and lean against the doorway, frowning and crossing my arms. She glances to me and holds up her hand for me to be quiet.

As if I need to be told. No shit.

Affair with Lana or no, Marchand would flip if he found out I was here. But now I really want to tell him. And all I'd have to do is start talking, ask Meagan if she wants those eggs, say it loud enough and this will all be over.

Meagan's shoulders slump and she mutters, "No, I don't think you planned it or lied. I'm sorry, I'm just frustrated, Bryan." She listens and since I can't hear his voice, he's not yelling.

What the fuck is he telling her?

He knew it was a holiday.

No way he forgot.

I've wondered probably more than she has, if he keeps her as his floor manager simply because she does a great job and he'd be hard-pressed to find someone better. But my instincts have shot that idea to the ground every time. I know it's more than that. He loves the game. The power trip. Why do guys like him do any of the shit they do? Because someone lets them, that's why. I'm so close to blowing this thing wide open. I'm about to say something when she hangs up.

Her hand is shaking as it combs through her hair. I exhale, realizing she needs me to make her feel better, not tip the boat over with us in it.

I walk to her and slip my arms around her naked body from behind, pulling her in close and kissing her shoulder. "You have to go in?"

"Yes. The computer system is acting up."

"You have time for eggs?"

She sighs, "He can wait while I have breakfast."

Nibbling on her, I murmur, "That's right. Because I'm a terrible cook and I need to show you how bad."

This makes her laugh a little which I take advantage of by tickling her, and then some more, making her beg me to stop, a huge, beautiful grin returning to her face. "That's better. No frowning when you're around me, Boss." Pinching her ass, she yelps and bounds away from me. "Did that on purpose to watch your cute little tits jiggle."

She cries out, "I thought you said they weren't too small!"

"Said they were perfect. Didn't say they weren't small."

She cracks up. "You're fucking rude!!"

I chase her, both of us naked, around the kitchen. I freeze on one side, and she freezes, too. "Look at what I've got," I devilishly smile while wiggling my fingers.

She backs into a corner. "Please, don't! I'm very ticklish!"

"Which only makes me want to do it more."

"No!" She ducks and weaves and while I could have easily trapped her, I'm into the chase so I let her dash to the other side of the kitchen. "Meagan, if you really wanted to leave, door's right there. You just passed it. So I think you're enjoying this no matter what you say." Her eyelashes flutter, and she glances to her exit, shakes her head, biting her lip. "Oh, so you *want* me to tickle you?"

"I want to watch your muscles ripple and your huge cock swing around like that. That's what I want."

At the mention of it, my flattered cock jumps to attention. "Oh really? What else do you want?"

"Not what…who," she smiles.

Annnnnnnd now I'm hard. "It's me or the eggs. We don't have time for both."

"Eggs."

Laughing I straighten up and head for the refrigerator, which is right next to where she's standing. But I act detached, ready to make breakfast.

She grabs my length and I lift an eyebrow. "What's this

you're doing? Thought you were hungry."

"I can grab something on the road," she giggles, looking softer than she does on most days.

I, being a man, love it.

It makes me want to draw her in and lose myself in her softness.

Melt into her.

For years.

"Come here, beautiful."

"I need to brush my teeth," she whispers after I try and slip her my tongue.

"I don't care about your breath, Meagan. Do you have any idea of the stuff I've tasted in my life?"

"But…you need to brush yours, too."

I crack up laughing, bend down, throw her over my shoulder and head for her bathroom. "Okay, I bet you have a whole department store of dental hygiene stuff in there. Let's get this done." I smirk, slapping her ass.

She moans, bouncing on my shoulder as I stroll along with Aslan following us. "Does he have to go out?"

"We got home late. He's good for how long this is going to take."

"And how long is that?"

Sliding her down my body, I whisper in her ear, "You're the one who has to work."

She sighs before spinning and dipping to her cabinet below the sink. She rises and we hold a look in the mirror's reflection. It's the first time we've seen us together. From her expression she's shocked by the image, too. We look like the perfect couple. Her eyelashes flutter nervously, so I slide my hands around her waist and on her stomach. "Don't future-fuck yourself."

She gives me a confused smile. "What?"

"Thinking too far ahead into the future. Let's just take this one step at a time. The only thing you've gotta do now is unscrew that lid off and slug a mouthful. Then hand it to me."

She does what I said, then I slug and the two of us stare at each other in the mirror with chipmunk cheeks, sloshing the painfully minty liquid around for as long as we can hack it. She bends over and spits it out, which presses her ass into my erection. I grind against her while she rinses and she sighs from how good it feels. I lean over and spit. She reaches behind her and grabs my shaft, shooting a building fire into my groin.

"We need some privacy, buddy," I tell Aslan and shut the door as I reach around and finger Meagan. Her eyelids grow heavy and she bends forward, arching her ass up. I lock eyes with her in the mirror as I enter her from behind. Groaning at how tight and slippery she is, I grab her hips and push in deeper. Her lips part as she watches me in the reflection.

"When I see you behind the bar tonight, I'm going to remember this." Her eyes close as I slide in deep and pick up the pace. "Oh, God, you feel so good inside me."

My teeth grit together. "When you're walking around the dining room, Boss, I'll be thinking of how much I love your pussy. When you catch me staring at you, that's what I'll be thinking. And it'll be hard to walk."

She laughs which makes her pussy contract and I groan under the heat it sends into me. "Oh God," she moans, arching her ass up higher and moving with me. Giving me her profile she offers her mouth for a kiss. I latch onto it and everything goes primal.

31

MEAGAN

Predictably it's a holiday zoo tonight at Le Marchand. I've already snaked Mira's flask out of her purse while she was seating a wealthy family of four. I had to do the same for one of the bussers. Everyone's on edge knowing tonight was destined for insanity. I get it. But I need them sober and alert!

Bryan's back from New Orleans, shouting in the kitchen as though that will solve our problems. The other chefs are moving fast but not fast enough for the whip-cracker. He's barking so loudly I run in and whisper-yell, "We can hear you in the dining room!"

He glares at me and shouts, "Get out of my kitchen!"

I hiss, "Like I was ever in it!" turning on my heel and fuming back into the throng. As soon as I become visible to the guests I plaster a perfect smile on my face and walk more slowly, and with more composure than I feel.

Cathy is at the far station making drinks for the servers

since she's faster than Lana. Jeremy is always on the far right, closer to the kitchen's door where I can spend the most time with him, though I've never given away that it's the reason I always station him there. So Lana is at the center of the bar tonight, and she glances to me as I walk out. I meet her eyes after looking at Jeremy and see the concern she's feeling. I nod to her and she gets back to work. The bar is five deep, and everyone wants a drink. It's the night of keeping Moms happy, which often makes Dads nervous, the perfect prescription for more booze.

Jeremy glances to me as I walk past. He gives me a wink and I know what he's thinking. A deep blush fills my cheeks and I regain my real smile.

It's been like this for the last three hours. So many errors coming from the kitchen, a dozen dishes sent back at the wrong temperature or things missing from plates, like fucking mashed potatoes. How do you forget the side dish on an entrée you've cooked a hundred times? The chefs are losing their shit with Bryan riding them so hard.

And then I'll see Jeremy and everything will feel good again. Right. Like nothing else matters.

I rush into the kitchen trying to appease a disappointed guest, the potato-less plate in my hands. "Philippe, forget something?" He grabs it, slaps a wad of mashed down and hands it back. "That looks terrible."

Bryan's attention is caught and a volcano erupts. "What the fuck? I'm surrounded by idiots! Philippe, did someone drop you as a child?"

My heart drops as I stare, remembering the day he texted that to me. What was I thinking, sleeping with him?

"And you!" he shouts at Lewis, the food runner. "How the fuck did you take that to a table? You're fired!"

I throw my arm up, pointing toward the dining room. "You can't fire him right now! We're bursting at the seams!"

Lewis is frozen as fresh dishes are slammed onto the steel counters for him to take out. Nobody knows what to do. The chefs are glancing to each other.

Bryan shouts, "You do it!"

"Me?" I cry out. "Who's going to watch the floor?"

His eyeballs bulge. "FUCK!!!!"

"Get ahold of yourself!" I hiss at him. "This is Mother's Day, Bryan! There are *families* out there!"

He snarls and points at Lewis. "What are you waiting for? Those plates won't carry themselves!"

Lewis is shaking, but he's a pro. He grabs the right napkins and special spoons for the dishes he has to take, and off he goes. The other runner races into the kitchen past him, his face saying that he heard the chaos and is going to keep a low profile.

I throw Bryan a disgusted glare and he sneers at me on

my way back out. "You're ridiculous!"

"Watch yourself, Meagan!"

I flip him off before I'm visible to the main room, dropping my hand and smiling again at the crowd. I walk past the bar. Jeremy glances over and gives me a look. He crooks a finger and rushes to whisper in my ear, "You can do this, Boss. Keep your head up."

Tension slides off me. My smile becomes real and I catch Lana watching me again. Why does she keep doing that? She's looked at me more tonight than she ever has. Am I imagining it?

Finally the night slows as time ticks toward a later hour when families want to be home on a Sunday.

No more on the waiting list.

No more mistakes.

No more screaming.

Hidden in the farthest server station, I cover my face and take deep breaths. Now that it's over I want to break down and laugh like a lunatic, or sob, just so I can release all the damn tension.

"Hey," his deep voice interrupts my mini-breakdown.

"You came to check on me?"

"Yeah. I saw you slink back here and thought you might need this." He pulls me in for a hug and I burrow into his chest. He tightens and hugs me with all of himself.

"Heads up," Mira whispers as she passes.

Jeremy and I separate quickly and he drops to the ground, scooping up coffee grinds with his hand while I tell him, "Get a dustpan and a broom!"

Bryan appears as Jeremy mutters, "Sorry boss. Where are they?"

"In dry storage. Go!"

He tosses the grinds from his cupped hand into the trash and mumbles, "Sorry," again.

Bryan steps to the right to make room for his exit, blue eyes locking onto me as soon as we're alone. "Why isn't he behind the bar?"

"Someone wanted Irish Coffee."

"I said no Irish drinks! We're a *French* restaurant."

"I know," I shrug, heart beating way too fast. "I'll remind him. But you can't say no to a guest, especially tonight when there have been so many mistakes. And it's just Jameson and coffee. We're not raising the Irish flag or anything."

He glares at me and jams his nubby finger in the tense air. "I want to see you in my office after closing tonight." He storms away and I grab onto the counter to steady myself.

My legs are shaking.

He might find out about us soon.

I saw how Lana was staring. She knows.

242

Mira, too, apparently. She wasn't surprised. Just warned us.

But Bryan can't find out tonight.

That would be the worst timing.

We've got an hour until closing and then we'll all clean up, I'll get bitched at, there might be screaming, but at least we'll be alone when it happens and I can tell him what I really think of him.

And then I'll go home and get the best night of sleep I've ever had. And it will be in Jeremy's arms.

I just have to get through this last hour.

And I need coffee to do it. Good thing I'm here.

32

JEREMY

Lana eyes me as I return to the bar. "Get caught?" she whispers.

"Caught doing what?" I casually ask.

She eyes me but then a cacophony of voices turns our attention to the front door. My eyes go wide and I burst out laughing as my whole fucking family pours into the restaurant. Mom and Dad and four of my brothers—Jaxson, Jake, Jason and Justin, and their wives and children. Too many cute little kids to count. Everyone's locked on me as they spot me across the elegant room. Most have their arms in the air, especially the children.

"JEREMY!"

"UNCLE JEREMY!!!"

Then the biggest surprise explodes out from where he was hiding behind the group, Jett, my biker brother who's always on the road and who we rarely see, is the surprise guest. "Look who's in Georgia!" he shouts, oblivious to the upper class, subdued conversations around him. "Hey little brother! Bet ya didn't expect to see my handsome mug, did ya?"

Laughing and strolling out from behind the bar I head over to say hello. My eyes dart quickly around, searching for Meagan. I want her to meet everyone.

Bryan is storming away from where he almost caught us, and his eyes lock on me, then flit to my family. His expression changes as he recognizes my father, Congressman Michael Cocker and my brother, Senator Justin Cocker. He immediately smoothes down his chef coat, his eyes locking onto me as he realizes I'm related to them.

Guess he never put that together before.

Meagan walks out from the server station and we lock eyes as I draw my family back near the host stand where there's room to hug everyone. I grab tow-headed little Hannah and set her on my hip as my brothers clap me on the back in man-hugs. Dad's hands are stuffed in his pockets, but he looks proud. Mom squeezes me and touches Hannah's cheek with a soft look in her eyes. This pretty little niece is the one I'm closest to, since Aslan has been her playmate many days. She and I both have something in common, both feel a little on the outside.

"What are you guys doin' here?" I grin.

Dad announces, looking handsome and sophisticated in a fine suit, "It's your mother's special day and since you had to work she wanted to bring the party to you."

I beam at her pretty face, "Mom, you cancelled the BBQ for me?"

Jason calls out, "Which means I don't get my fresh ginger-ale! So you better be flattered."

I laugh as Mom waves his remark away. "You haven't invited us to see your new job! And I wanted to have *all* my boys together, since I so rarely get to these days." Her eyes are filled with love as they travel across all of our faces.

Sarah, bouncing their child on her hip, slaps his arm as Jason calls out, "But I bet they don't have Mom's chili here."

"Oh, Jason, be quiet," Mom mutters.

"They sure don't," I chuckle. "Jett, where's your wife?"

"In my pocket," he smirks, then rolls his eyes, admitting, "I wish! I'm in hers. Honey Badger's lady is popping out a baby and she wanted to be there to help. They hired a mid-wife to come to the house. She called Mom and asked if she would mind."

Nancy Cocker waves her hand like it's totally fine. "What better Mother's Day present than to *become* a mother? She should be there for her friend, and she promised to bring Sofia to see me soon. I need my grandchildren around me more often!"

"There aren't enough here?" Justin smirks.

"Hey Jett," I smile, glancing to our father. Seeing them in the same room together is a fucking miracle since they don't get along, polar opposites with a lot of bad blood between them. "What'd you do, slip Dad a pot brownie so he'd relax and let you come to the party?"

Justin shakes his head, "Tsk tsk tsk."

Jason and Jake make hissing and Oooooooo noises.

Jaxson, the oldest and always the rock, cocks an eyebrow at me, smiling with respect that I called out the pink elephant in the room.

Dad, he just grumbles to himself without actually making a sound.

Jett cracks up which is what I wanted.

"Had to poke the bear, didn't you?" Mom sighs.

"Where's Grams?"

"There were some women at her Senior Living who were spending the evening playing Gin Rummy since they didn't have visitors. She wanted to win some money. Said to send her love."

"I'll give her a call tomorrow. Let's get you guys to a table. Mira! Somewhere close to the bar. Everyone, this is our hostess, isn't she pretty?"

Jakes' wife, Drew, rocks Ethan with a smile. "Oh, are you two dating? I heard you have a woman here you like."

I laugh, "Where'd you hear that?" eyeing Jake, who shoves his hands in his pockets and looks away. "And from the lack of surprise on everyone's faces, I'm guessing word got around."

Justin slips his arm around his wife's back and she gazes up at him. "We've given up on trying to stop the grape vine. It was me who told everyone."

"What?!!"

"Sorry."

"Well, *you* told *me*," Drew, the only one with a true Southern drawl, says to Jake, "Justin didn't. It was you, when you came home from having beers together."

"Baby, you're not supposed to rat me out." Jake goes to slap her ass, but Dad grabs his arm.

"We're in a public dining establishment."

"*Establishment?*" Jett mutters, mocking the snooty word.

"Don't start," Jaxson tells him.

His wife, Rachel, tells our hostess with a warning look, "Lead the way. We've got hungry kids and the adults are worse."

Mom takes Dad's hand, and he relaxes a little.

Justin hits his twin's shoulder so hard that he pushes Jason off balance. "And if this *jackass* doesn't eat fast no one's food is safe."

Mom rolls her eyes, "Since Grams isn't here to say it, I will."

But we all say it with her: "Language!" And everyone cracks up.

What an amazing clusterfuck this will be. I wave over two of the bussers and they come running. "Can you put three tables together? And get some highchairs? I've gotta get back to the bar. Cathy's waving at me."

"You got it, Jeremy."

I hand Hannah to her dad and tell my family, "Guys, I have to get back to work. Try not to get me fired. No fighting."

33

JEREMY

The restaurant is only half full now. You can finally hear the ambient classical music playing in the background. I jump behind the bar and say, "Sorry, ladies."

"Totally okay, hon," Cathy calls over. "Those all your nieces and nephews?"

"Yep. One's not here tonight. And you can see one's on the way."

"So cute! How does that little redhead carry that huge belly?"

"Ask Jason. He keeps knocking her up."

Next to me Lana is checking out my brothers and their wives with intense interest.

I throw a balled up napkin at her. "Your mouth's hanging open."

She snaps it shut, whipping her long hair over her shoulder to cut a quick look my way.

"What?"

"Nothing. We're doing our show for them, right?"

A grin spreads from deep within. Hadn't thought of it, yet, but now that she's brought it up, I know they're going to love it. "Yeah, but not yet. I'll say when. Pass it on."

She nods and slips the bottle she was pouring away before she walks to whisper in Cathy's ear. I get a nod and the three of us go back to normal until the time is right.

Meagan appears behind me, dropping off a box of cocktail straws that we don't need. She whispers, "One of your brothers looks so much like you."

"That's Jake."

"Jake." She repeats like she's storing it in her memory to remember who's who amongst the five of them.

"Yep. He's the next one up."

"You're the youngest?"

"Yep!"

"Like Devin."

We lock eyes and I touch her fingertips before she slips out from behind the bar and heads for the host stand. My family is settling in at their joined tables, laughing and caught in separate conversations.

I look over and catch Jake watching Meagan's journey through the restaurant. His eyes shoot over to meet mine and his eyebrows cock up. Not too obvious, just a little. We've been grabbing beers every week for over a month now, and I've told him a little about her and our walks. He tried to dig for why I wasn't making a move and I asked him to drop it. When he pressed, I told him she used to date the owner. He didn't ask again.

I tip my head to tell him she's the one. An approving smile lights his dark eyes and he turns to his wife and whispers in her ear. Motherfucker is telling her right now, isn't he? I'm gonna kill him.

Mom seated herself so she's facing me, and her eyes keep traveling my way as I make drinks and talk to the guests. Even with the dining room count dwindling, the bar is full. There are a lot of people in this world without a mom to celebrate anymore, and this holiday hurts them. The media doesn't realize that, when they're shoving gift ideas down your throat. It just makes you want to chase it with booze.

The guy serving my family is new, came from an upscale restaurant near Lenox Mall, and he recognizes Mom and Dad from when they've dined there, and they remember him, too. He grins and shakes hands with them, compliments Mom's beautiful new necklace Dad gave her, and everyone loosens up even more, checking out the menus and discussing what the children can eat. God it feels good to see them all here.

I want them to see me in action back here.

I want them to *stop* worrying.

I want them to know…I'm back.

I'm alive. I need them to believe it. And I need to feel it, myself, and start my new life as a part of them again. I miss my family. I'm done keeping them at a distance. Even with their quirks, like being terrible at keeping secrets, I love every single one of them. They're my blood.

After the new guy gathers everyone's food order into his iPhone App, he vanishes into the kitchen. I lock eyes with Meagan across the room while pouring a Chopin vodka and soda for Viola, one of our steady regulars who always sits in front of me. Meagan catches onto what I'm about to do, and she touches Mira, turning her attention, too.

My family is engaged in conversations. I call out in my deepest register, really bringing the military aspect home, "What. Time. Is. It."

Everyone looks over.

Lana and Cathy shout, with severe faces, "SHOW. TIME. SIR!"

The dining room stills and everyone present turns in their chairs to watch. I wink at my Mom and BOOM.

It's on.

The girls and I go through the drill. Our faces show no emotion as we toss glinting liquor bottles high in the air one after the other. The performance seamlessly executes. Not a drop spilled. And when we pour the martinis with their impressively long streams into the chilled glasses, my family goes nuts with applause and cheering, especially Hannah who's tiny voice is screaming, "Woohoo!!! Uncle Jeremy!!!"

Lana surprises me with, "Congressman, this is for you," setting her martini on the bar with a smile. Guess she recognized him. Or she's the one who's been whispering in Meagan's ear about my family. I bet that's why she was staring at them.

Cathy follows the cue. "Mrs. Cocker, I made this for you. Your son here is pretty great. You did well."

A grin breaks out on my face and I flush beet red, setting the martini I made down and telling our black sheep, "Jett, this is all yours. Thanks for making the trip from Louisiana."

"Awwww!" The entire restaurant starts clapping, many whispering amongst themselves.

"Happy Mother's Day, Mom," I call out.

She's got tears in her eyes. She jumps up and runs over to me. I walk out from behind the bar, lift her up in a big hug and kiss her hair. "Oh, Jeremy, I love you so much."

"I'm back, Ma," I whisper to her.

She grabs my face with both hands and shakes my head like she can't squeeze it hard enough. Too choked up to speak she just smacks my cheeks a couple times, grabs one of my arms and heads back to the table, shaking her pretty head along the way and covering her mouth with her hand.

Meagan has walked closer, and is now standing in the middle of the dining room. I glance over to her. She's smiling with incredible warmth at me. I cock my head to call her over and she hesitates, but hurries her footsteps, glancing to the kitchen. I do a quick look around to see if Bryan's watching. He ain't, so fuck him.

"Guys!" I call out to my family who is talking amongst themselves again. The adults turn around, and Hannah looks over, too. The younger kids are busy being children. I hold my index finger over Meagan, pointing downward at the top of her head. "Memorize this face."

It dawns on them what I'm saying.

I'm claiming her.

Meagan looks up, sees my finger and grabs it, looking happy more than embarrassed as she shakes her head for me to stop it. I wrestle it back, hold it in front of my lips to let them know it's a secret, but Jett sticks two in his lips and wolf whistles.

The new guy runs out like a dog called to heel. "Yes?"

My whole family cracks up, including me.

34

MEAGAN

As I float into the kitchen Bryan charges out from behind the burners and grabs my arm. "Did you know Jeremy was related to them?"

"To who? You're squeezing my arm too hard!" I try to yank it back but he's stronger than I am.

"The politicians, Meagan! The politicians!"

"I knew he was the Senator's brother. Justin was here at the pre-opening party. You met him! Let go of my arm!"

He grunts and releases me. Pacing, with the other chefs eyeing him without his knowledge, Bryan runs his hand through his famous hair, eyes locked on the kitchen floor. "All this time I've been treating him like a nothing and…" He lunges at me and grabs both my arms this time, though not as painfully because now he wants something. "We're going to go out there and you're going to introduce me!"

"Okay!"

I've done this a million times since we opened, brought him to tables who didn't know him and introduced the man who made their delicacies…but this one I'm not looking forward to.

Lewis starts to run the first of their appetizers out but I stop him and take the two best dishes. "Grab the others." To Bryan I say, "Take these and I'll announce that you're the chef."

"I'm the owner, not *just* the chef."

"And I'm the manager, not just the…oh, wait. I'm not a chef at all." I cock my head with heavy sarcasm and hand him the dishes. He takes them, his patience with me, gone.

I lift two more dishes, glance to the seating chart and memorize who they go to. Shit, this lobster bisque is for Jeremy's mother. Holding my head high I tell Bryan, "The crab cakes are for the Congressman."

"Perfect," he mutters.

As I pass the bar on the left and see Jeremy chatting the bar regulars, my neck straightens and a real smile spreads from within.

He just pointed me out to his family and said, *Memorize her.*

When Bryan and I dated he never told anyone. And he certainly never made me this happy.

I set the bisque down and say, "Mrs. Cocker. This

bowl is hot." She looks up, her brown eyes so like her son's. "What's your name?"

"Meagan Forrester."

She's about to say something but I can feel Bryan waiting for me to introduce him, and this is the meal he cooked with care.

One thing I will never fault him is his skill, and I don't want those crab cakes cold.

So I smile quickly to her and straighten up to announce to the table, "Everyone, I want to introduce the chef and owner of Le Marchand, Bryan Marchand."

They nod and murmur hellos and also their appreciation for the atmosphere and decor. Senator Cocker stands and shakes his hand. "I met you at the grand opening."

Bryan beams at him, blue eyes shimmering like a star. He shakes the extended hand and smiles, "Of course! You were sitting with the Governor. How is he?"

"Great. He and I are having dinner here next Thursday."

"I'll make sure I come out and say hello. And this is your father?"

"Dad?" Justin smiles, sliding his hands in his pocket with class. As Bryan shakes Mr. Cocker's hand and chats about whatever, Justin meets my eyes with a smirk. I blink and he glances to his raven-haired wife and she nods to me with the same look. It dawns on me that Bryan didn't ask to be introduced to her. Only to the men in power. What a fatal error. And they are letting me in on the secret that they know he's an asshole.

I hear Bryan saying, while people begin eating, "Your son has been an excellent addition to my team, Congressman."

Michael Cocker sits as he says, "I'm not surprised."

Bryan smiles and nods, motioning to Jeremy. This gives me an excuse to look over at him. He's behind the bar, watching and listening. "His work ethic is outstanding. Always on time and doing more than is asked of him."

I almost snort as Jeremy cocks an eyebrow at me, clearly thinking of having sex with me last night. That was more than Bryan asked of him, for sure.

"Please let me know if I can be of assistance in any way. Meagan, let's let them enjoy their meals."

"Great meeting you," Jeremy's mother says to Bryan, holding out her hand like, *Did you forget it's not my husband's day, dumbass?* But her face is very elegant even as she cuts his lack of manners to shreds with a smile.

Bryan falters and takes her hand.

"Are you one of his daughters?"

I almost vomit.

She chuckles and then eyes me with a knowing smile. "Meagan, I can't wait to learn *all* about you."

A flush stains my cheeks as I hastily ask the table, "Does everyone have everything they need?"

The beautiful blonde child Jeremy was carrying meets my eyes and asks, "Are you and Uncle Jeremy in love?"

My jaw drops and a lot of them start laughing. I cut a look to Bryan's face as his eyes sharpen. Jeremy is acting like he didn't hear that, his head down as he turns to run a guest's credit card.

"I'm his boss, so yes, I do care about him. Your uncle is a very good man. Excuse me."

Bryan and I go to leave, and I think I covered that up well. Nobody can fault a child for saying something crazy. They do it all the time.

But then one of his brothers, I don't know his name but he's beefy and blond, and not one of the twins. He calls after me, "Oh, you're his boss alright!"

Oh.

My.

God.

35

MEAGAN

My face goes tight as I see Bryan realizing what's really going on, his face the color of lava. He's on my tail as I rush into the kitchen before he blows up in front of everyone.

The second we're inside he grabs my arm much harder than he did before. "Ow!" I cry out.

In a voice filled with venom and low so that it doesn't leave this room he snarls, "You and Jeremy?!! For how long!"

I beg him, "Bryan, let go of me!" His fingers are digging into my veins. "It just started! You're hurting me! Let go!"

Alberto hisses from behind the line, "Bryan, man, let go of her arm!"

That just angers him more. He tightens his grip and gives it a hard yank, pulling me so that I'm bending to the side with him looming over me like a monster. "Have you been fucking that guy right under my nose?!"

Jeremy walks into the kitchen and when he sees what's happening he lunges for Bryan and shouts, "GET OFF HER!"

My arm is released and I careen backwards to get away from them. Bryan spins around and Jeremy punches him in the face so hard blood splatters, wavy hair floating in the air before Bryan lands on the ground. Jeremy steps over him to get to me, furious as he cups my face. "You okay, baby?"

"Yes!" I gasp.

Lana rushes in, screams, "Bryan!" and falls to her knees by him.

"He knows."

"I figured," Jeremy mutters, looking at my arm. "Jesus, I'm gonna kill him."

Having heard their brother shouting, his five brothers crash through the kitchen door. Bryan doesn't see them because he's livid and bleeding and his eyes are locked on Jeremy's back.

Before I can warn Jeremy he's coming, Jake grabs Bryan's chef coat by the shoulder blades, spins him around and punches him so hard he hits the floor cold. The brothers surround his limp body like the handsomest human cage that ever existed, legs spread.

Jeremy's nostrils are flaring and he nods to them.

His father strolls into the kitchen, the picture of

elegant sophistication. He takes a look around and eyeballs Bryan, then says to his son the senator, "Justin, you can't keep doing things like this. You're a public servant now."

"He was attacking Jeremy from behind, Dad!"

The congressman frowns, grey eyes dropping once more to Bryan who's groaning on the floor. "A coward's move," he mutters with disdain. Walking to the line, he introduces himself to the chefs. "Gentlemen, my apologies."

"You don't have to worry, Congressman," Alberto informs him with a tone that says he's had enough. "It won't leave this kitchen."

"Thank you." He turns around and nods to me. "I'm sorry we jeopardized your job. We didn't know you and my son were a secret."

Jeremy's back straightens. "It's not like that, Dad."

I slip my hand into Jeremy's. His fingers tighten around mine.

The congressman points at Bryan and asks me, "Were you dating Marchand?"

The brothers are all watching me.

"Not really, but in a way, yes, sir."

How do you explain booty call without sounding like a slut?

"Was it still going on when you and my son…?" He trails off.

"No."

Jeremy's chest puffs up. "No, Dad! But since you're asking, I did try to steal her from him and I don't regret it."

My eyes cut to his profile and I gaze at him, surprised. He squeezes my fingers but keeps his eyes locked on his father. With how he's standing so straight and proud, he looks so much like the Marine that he is.

Congressman Cocker says, "Jeremy. I'm talking to Meagan." His sharp eyes lock back onto me. "Did my son try to steal you?"

"Maybe? Honestly, until just now, I didn't know that he was purposefully doing that."

"And you care about him."

I smile. "Very much."

Pointing at Bryan again, Mr. Cocker asks, "This guy is an asshole, isn't he?"

I blink and nod, "Yes, sir."

The brothers all laugh under their breaths, shifting their weight and relaxing now that they know their dad has been messing with us all, just to have a little fun.

The beefy blonde says, "Careful Dad. Thought you hated cuss words!"

"There is a time and a place, Jerald," he replies with an amused gleam in his eyes before he disappears into the dining room.

Jeremy turns to me with a growing grin. "Did you see that? He was playing us."

"He reminds me of you. Unfortunately."

Jeremy's eyes glitter and he shrugs, "You love it," turning to his brothers.

The beefy brother mutters to himself, "I fuckin' hate that he still calls me that."

"Jett, when are you going to let it go and just accept it?" Jake asks.

Justin's twin says, "It's never going to stop."

Justin agrees, "He's *always* going to call you by Grandpa's name."

The sandy-brown haired brother who must be Jaxson, the one Lana told me about—his voice is deep and calm as he tells Jett, "Maybe it's about time you took it as a compliment."

Bryan groans and everyone looks down at him. Lana strokes his hair and asks, "You okay, baby?"

I gasp and Jeremy makes a face, muttering to me, "Yeah, so they're doin' it."

I stare at him and whisper, "What the fuck?"

"I'm not a snitch."

"Jeremy!"

Bryan rises on his elbows and peers at his human cage. "Great," he mutters, admitting defeat.

265

Jeremy kneels and locks eyes with Bryan. "You ever lay a hand on Meagan again and you'll pick up your teeth with broken fingers."

Bryan snarls, "You're fired."

"I quit, you fuckin' piece of shit."

"You're going to jail!"

I hold up the darkening mark and announce, "Call the cops and I'll show them my arm, and then I'll be more than happy to inform them you tried to attack him when Jeremy came to my defense."

Bryan's eyes narrow in fury. He's still on the ground and doesn't see how he's going to be allowed up with this wall of muscle around him.

Lana rises and backs away, realizing she's been betting on a losing horse.

The brothers move to let me into their circle. Jeremy stands at my side as I tell my tormentor, "And I quit, too, you sonofabitch."

Lewis's voice interrupts, "So, what about your entrees?"

"Oh shit. I'm Jason, by the way," Justin's twin says to me. "So, we're starving. And our mom's out there probably cursing the day she didn't have daughters, again. Should we just take off and find some fast food place that's open or can we stay and enjoy our meal?"

Jett chuckles deep and low. "Yeah, what now?"

I lock eyes with Bryan. He snarls, "No way."

Lana walks over to my side. Now I'm flanked by her and Jeremy. She throws her hands on her hips and says, "You're seriously going to throw away your reputation by making that family eat somewhere else? Do you know how many wealthy Buckhead residents are out there with cell phones?"

He deflates. "Fine. Eat."

Jeremy takes my hand. "Join us?"

Justin calls over with an amused smirk to the chefs. "I trust you won't spit in our food."

Alberto's eyes dance as he cocks an eyebrow. "That depends. Is Bryan sitting with you?"

My jaw drops and I glance to Bryan, who's also shocked.

Alberto's voice drops to a severe timber as he informs his boss, "We're walking out as soon as this place closes tonight, Marchand. Find yourself a new kitchen. We're done. Until then, guys, you ready to do your best work?"

Mutual agreements all around.

Alberto asks me, "Meagan, what can we make for you?"

Smiling, I say, "Sea Bass please. Thank you."

"Any time. And I mean that. You go somewhere? I'll

come with you."

Blushing with gratitude I nod to Alberto and feel a tug on my hand. Jeremy leads me out to the dining room for the first time as a guest.

The brothers let Lana walk out in front of them, ever the gentlemen, so I hear her mutter right behind me, "I have the worst luck with men."

Jake hears her and says, "I have some cousins I could introduce you to."

Jeremy gives my fingers a quick squeeze with a look that says he's never gonna let that happen.

36

JEREMY

"Where do you want this crappy, flower painting?" I call to my wife.

She pokes out her head from our kitchen and gives me an impatient look. "It's a beautiful work of art, Jeremy."

Smirking at her I hold it up. "Where do you want the fluff piece, Boss?"

"Stop calling me that! I'm not your boss anymore," she sighs. "I'm your partner. We invested equally in this restaurant, so we are equals."

"I like you above me in status, baby. Makes getting you below me in bed all the more challenging." I set the canvas down and pull her to my body. "Why must you argue with me when you know it makes me hard?"

She laughs and kisses me, slipping her fingers into my hair. "You don't like the new paintings?"

"Meh."

"But it was your idea to feature local artists."

"Doesn't mean I'm going to like them all."

Cecily's voice echoes in from the back entrance of our six-month-young, surprisingly popular, gluten-free leaning, lounge-bar-restaurant fusion thingy that we named Crash. I thought it up after two weeks of us searching for the right name while we haggled with the previous owner to throw the liquor license in with the price.

When Meagan asked, "Why Crash?"

I told her, "It's how we met."

Sold. We hired a designer to work with Meagan on how she wanted the place to look since I have no design skills what so ever.

Then Jake and his men did the construction on it. Uncle Don was totally on board with him taking on the side project since we're family. Besides, he was like everyone else, happy I found someone who made me happy and woke me back up.

It's nothing grand and inaccessible like Le Marchand was, which is no longer in business by the way. We heard Bryan went back to France where he could be appreciated.

Crash has half the tables and half the ceiling height, and no fucking old-school chandeliers that could hurt anyone if they fell. It's darkly lit, intimate and comfy with loads of throw pillows in the bar section's booths, tea lights and succulent plants on all the dining tables, serving comfort food that Meagan has dreamed up with the help of Alberto, by people in black jeans and black halters and tank tops. Every time Jaxson, Rachel, Sylvia, and Ben come down from his ranch he calls it, hip.

But hipsters have sullied that word a bit so I don't like it. I like to call it…our first baby.

"Guys? You here?" Cess calls again.

"Keep walking!" Meagan shouts, right in my ear.

I make a face and wiggle my finger in it. "Jeeeeezus."

She laughs and smacks my ass before turning to greet her sister who's walking into the main room with Kevin holding her hand, his arm at full extension since he's only three and a half. Meagan dips down and lifts him up. "Hi little buddy!"

"Hiiiiiii Germy!" he waves at me.

"He likes you more than me," she grumbles.

Ignoring her I smile at him, "Hey, Kev, you get a haircut, little man? Decide to wear carrots to spruce it up?"

Cecily starts picking the orange pieces out. "He always throws his food around. I'm hoping he grows out of it. Oh, that's beautiful!" she says as her eyes land on the flower painting. "I love that! How much?"

"One dollar," I mutter.

Meagan rolls her eyes. "Jeremy hates it."

"What? Why?" Cecily stares at the piece. "It's so pretty!"

"He's a guy," Meagan mutters, setting Kevin down. "With horrible taste." She picks up the canvas and carries it to the wall opposite my bar. "And it's only here for two weeks before we switch it out for someone's else work. How about here?"

I wave my hand back and forth. "Oh no, you don't!"

Her eyebrows fly up with fake innocence. "What? This is great! You can admire it every night while you're working. See?"

"Ha ha and no. How 'bout we put it in the bathroom. That way when I take a shit I'll have inspiration."

You know what I love about my wife? She hung the damn thing in the men's room.

37

MEAGAN

Cathy waves goodbye to us as Jeremy locks up. He calls over his shoulder to her while turning the key, "You kicked ass tonight!"

She laughs, "Did you see that guy begging for my number?"

"Which one?" I smile.

"Very funny. You know that hasn't happened since this." She points to her eight-months-pregnant belly. "Although my boobs sure are bigger now. Guess that's why you guys keep me around now that I'm moving slower, huh? Hey, are we having brunch at your house tomorrow, or are you guys coming to our house?"

"You're coming over!" I lace my fingers with my husband's as we head to our Jeep. "Eleven o'clock. Just you guys. We can't fit anyone else."

Jeremy squeezes my hand. "Hey."

"Well, we can't."

Climbing in her Nissan, Cathy puts in her earbuds to listen Steve Martin's audio book on the way home. She's a huge fan of his, too. If he ever comes to Atlanta again, she and I will go see him. I missed him last time he was at the Fox Theater and have been kicking myself ever since.

Jeremy helps me up into the Jeep as he always does. "Thank you, handsome."

"You think my house is too small."

I knew there would be a discussion. Biting my lip I tell him, "Climb in. We'll talk about it on the way."

"We've already talked about it."

I tilt my head. Mr. Stubborn exhales through his nose and shuts my door, trudging around the hood and locking eyes with me through the windshield from under his pronounced brow. God, he can be so dramatic. As he starts the engine and slams the door I try very hard not to smile, and succeed. Leaning my elbow on my window I wait for us to leave the parking lot before starting.

I know he wants me to be the first to speak. He's too busy stewing in defensive juices.

As soon as we're on Piedmont, I steady myself and begin, "You know it was painful for me to sell my condo." I hold up my hand before he interrupts. "But I sold it because you already had the money saved up to invest in Crash, and I needed to put in my half."

"I never asked you to. I could have paid for it."

Locking eyes with him I gently remind him, "And like I've said before, then it would have been in essence *your* restaurant."

"We're married. Everything is ours."

"But it was my dream and I wanted to pay half. And if everything is ours, then why did you just say, you think my house is too small, not *our* house?"

His lips tighten.

I reach over and take his hand, which is not as malleable as usual. Time to employ a trick Rachel taught me.

This is the first healthy relationship I've ever been in, so I needed all the help I could get because when Jeremy and I got married less than a year after meeting, I was in over my head, crazy in love with him, but I had no tools.

So I called my sister-in-laws and gathered enough advice to write a book on marriage counseling. Since they have strong marriages with stubborn men, and they're all pretty strong-willed themselves, I knew I was asking in the right places.

Drew told me in her sweet drawl, "Only ask someone in a bad marriage what *not* to do. And if you do, do it discreetly. Most people can't tell you the truth anyway, because they don't want to know the reason things are going badly. They'd have to do something about it."

Of course my sister offered up her pearls, too, and I took notes, but asking Drew, Rachel, Jaimie, Sarah, and even Luna when I can get her on the phone, brought me closer into the family. Which I wanted so badly. Cecily is a big fan of them, too. She, Mike and Kevin come to all the family functions. As do my parents. It's become a real zoo.

So what Rachel taught me is not so much a trick but a way to get through to a man when he's heading into his man-cave. We love that they're so masculine, so it's mandatory to keep them that way. I don't want to cut his balls off, figuratively speaking. I like them too much. Non-figuratively speaking, too. And yes, I mean I want us to keep having sex. A lot.

I need to make him feel loved.

Let him know I'm not attacking him.

I am on his side.

Always.

That's what love is.

"I want you to know while we talk about this, that I love you. I want to discuss this sensitive topic so we can move on and be happy."

Jeremy glances to me, the sharp edges around his eyes softening. He shakes out his shoulders a little to release the building steam and mutters, "I love you, too. Okay, go."

"You've let me decorate your home and it's much cozier and I'm so happy with it." He meets my eyes like he doesn't believe me. "I am! I just have my heart on something bigger."

He huffs through his nose, struggling not to get defensive as he says, "We've been very happy in that house, baby. The dogs are happy. They love it there."

"Yes, but will the baby?"

Jeremy blinks away from the windshield. "Did you just say *baby*?"

Acting very casual I lean on my hand and stare off. "Because I was just wondering if we have enough space? I mean, sure, when it's a newborn we'll want it in our room. But what about when we start having sex again? Baby's gotta go!" I twist in my seat and very seriously say, "Do you understand my dilemma?"

Jeremy's frowning. He pulls the Jeep over and puts it in park, even hitting the emergency brake. "Meagan Cocker, are you telling me that you're pregnant?"

"Why else would I say our home is small?"

He blinks at me and starts shaking his head. "Oh man, I don't like you sometimes." Bursting into laughter he hits the dashboard and shouts, "Why'd I have to teach you how to fuck with me? You're better at it than I am now!"

"You're going to be a daddy, Jeremy."

His jaw clenches and his Adam's apple quivers. "When did you find out?"

"Before the shift today. It's why Cecily popped by. She brought the tests. We did three!"

His voice is hoarse with emotion as he asks, "Why didn't you tell me?" He's trying not to cry.

"I wanted to tell you when it was just us, when we could go home and celebrate alone. I didn't want everyone at Crash congratulating us until we had some time to be together and soak in it. And I had Cess do the tests with me because I always promised her I'd do that. Plus I didn't want to disappoint you if it was negative. It's very complicated, all this fertility stuff."

Jeremy bends over the gearshift to kiss me. He starts laughing with happiness mid-kiss and pulls away to shout, "We're gonna have a baby!"

I laugh and clap my hands, grinning, before he leans over and grabs my face. "God, I love you, Meagan. I love you so damn much I can hardly stand it sometimes."

With tears in my eyes I whisper, "You should have seen how mad you were getting."

He smiles, his eyes reddening. "I'm going to get you back."

"I think delivering the baby without meds will be payback enough."

He chuckles and kisses me, pulling back to murmur against my lips, "Fair enough."

38

JEREMY

Meagan waits for me to unlock the door, readying herself for the onslaught of love we're about to receive. Aslan and Noosh come bounding out of our house—Aslan to me and the small, tan and white, fluffy girl-dog I bought for Meagan, to her.

"Hello Noosh! How are you little love? Did you miss me? You did? Awwww!" She carries her into a home that, had you walked in a year ago, you wouldn't have recognized it.

It's like Better Homes & Gardens threw up in here.

I give her a hard time, but I secretly like all the homey improvements. Except for one picture that hangs above the espresso machine. It's supposed to be abstract but just looks like a blob to me. But whatever. As long as my wife is happy, I'm happy.

She sets down Noosh, pets Aslan and glances up to me

from where she's scratching behind his ears. "Are you thinking about the baby?"

I nod and pull her into the bedroom. The dogs try to follow but I bend and tell them, "We'll be back. You can't come in yet. Deal with it."

Their happy, panting mouths shut, and their heads tilt before I close the door.

I press Meagan against the nearest wall and she reacts with surprise. "Right here?"

"I wanted to fuck you in the living room but they stare at us and it's weird," I murmur, working hungry kisses down her neck. "I can't believe you're carrying our child. That's so fucking sexy."

"It excites me, too," she whispers, pulling my black tank top off over my head. "Every free chance I had to peek out into the bar tonight I was thinking how much I wanted to tell you…and how much I wanted to fuck you."

I devour her in a frenzied kiss, clawing my way down her legs and fumbling with urgency to unzip her black jeans. "Going to have to buy preggy-jeans for work."

She locks eyes with me. "I. Can't. Wait."

My cock reaches for her, painfully confined, and I groan and drop to my knees, hurrying to get her naked from the waist down. I throw her left thigh over my shoulder and separate her swelling folds with my fingers, diving my tongue in there and licking her while she rubs against it.

"Just like that, Jeremy," she moans, grabbing my head. "That's a good bartender."

I chuckle low and deep into her pussy and shove my tongue as far as I can get it inside her. Her moan heightens and her fingers claw at my head. "Yes!" She rubs her cunt against my mouth and my eyes roll back for how hot that is. She cries out and presses down. "Not deep enough," she whimpers. "More. I need your cock. I neeeeeeed you. Don't make me wait."

"Oh yeah?" I jump up and strip, taking a few steps back so she can watch. With hooded eyes my wife stares at my body like she's ravenous for it. I shove my jeans off and strip everything, even my watch.

"You're taking too long!" she moans.

Palming myself I rasp, "What do you want?"

"You!"

"Take off your shirt. Nice and slow. Good. That's right. Bra next. Slower. Yeah. That's it. Everything off. Even your necklace. Slide it to the ground there. Perfect. No, keep the wedding ring!"

Her eyes go wide as she leans against the wall, nude and wet. She reaches down between her legs and plays with herself. "You said everything."

"That rings stays. And keep touching yourself because

wow, that's fucking hot."

She begins to remove the ring, and I start for the bathroom. "Fine. We're done here."

Laughing she calls over, "Okay! The ring's on! Come back! I'm still married to you."

I eyeball her from the side and see her looking at my cock because from profile it's intimidating. "You like this?"

"I wish it were bigger."

I crack up and mutter, "Yeah right. Come here."

She releases her pussy and pads over to me, nice and slow while slipping her fingers in her mouth and sucking. My mouth slackens because she's never done that before.

I need to get her pregnant more often.

"What do you want me to do, *Boss?*" she smirks, turning the tables.

"Ooh, I like that," I rasp, stroking myself. "Hang on." I pick her up and throw her on the bed, standing in front of her. "I want to watch you make yourself cum."

Meagan's eyes flicker. "I can't do that. I've never done that before!" Off my look she corrects herself, "With someone watching! It's too scary."

"Too vulnerable, you mean."

"Yeah," she sighs, covering her face and crossing her legs.

My voice is thick with lust as I tell her, "Do it anyway."

She locks eyes with me, nervous, but her legs open a little. Then a little more. And a little more. She watches me staring at her moist pussy like I want to lick it. Her hand slides down and hovers over the mound.

"You throbbing, baby?"

She breathes, "Yes."

"You *want* to touch yourself, don't you?"

She smiles, "Yes," shyly biting her lip.

"Give your cunt a little touch for me, see how it feels."

Her fingers shiver downward and she touches the cleft just above and then dips down to inside her folds to tickle her clit with her finger. Her breath hitches. So does mine. I want to stroke myself but this is so fucking hot I know I'll cum before I want to.

My lips part as she slides her middle finger into herself and arches her hips a little up. She closes her eyes so she can block me out and then she starts to move her hips in a circle, slipping her fingers up and down her slit.

Our eyes lock and she a releases a shy moan. I can see her dripping, she's so wet from this. I groan and grab my cock, promising myself not to stroke it.

Meagan's eyelids get heavier and she moans louder with more courage and less shame. I watch her bringing herself to the edge and shake my head because I can't fucking take it anymore. I groan, struggling not to move, but it's useless. "I have to fuck you," I growl and climb onto her, plunging all of my strength between her legs. She hooks her legs around my ass and cries out as I fill her. She was so close to cumming that with my cock stretching her throbbing walls, she explodes and I yell out from how good her orgasm feels against me. She grabs my shoulder blades and our mouths crash together. Pounding her, I bring her quivering body to the edge one more time. We're moaning and fucking and writhing and changing positions until I can't hold back anymore.

As my cock thickens Meagan whispers, "You're going to be a daddy, Jeremy. We're going to be a family. I love you."

I lose it with the strongest orgasm I've ever felt. Tears fall down my face and I burrow into her neck to hide them. Instinctively she strokes my head.

"I wasn't happy until I met you," I rasp into her skin. "I was lost."

"I'm here, Jeremy. I'm not going anywhere."

Clutching her to me, I gasp for breath, stunned at the emotional breakdown I'm having. Never saw this coming. Didn't know all these emotions were so pent up.

We stay like this, with my face buried until I get a hold of myself. Then I kiss my wife and, trying to act like I didn't just lose my shit, I clear my throat. "I'm all good. I'm fine."

She's gazing at me with love. "I know. It's alright."

"We've gotta walk the dogs."

Her eyes flicker and she nods. "I almost forgot. Well, let's get it over with."

We get dressed in sweats and comfy shirts and I kiss her briefly and ask her, "You ready?"

"Yes."

Opening the door to the hallway we discover Aslan and Noosh sitting at attention with their leashes in their mouths, waiting for us.

Meagan and I break into laughter and she shrugs, "I guess they're ready too!"

"Ya think?" I laugh, slap her ass, and off we go. Our little family of four, that soon will be five.

EPILOGUE

MEAGAN

A little shy of 9 months later.

Drugged up to the nines with my hair matted to my face I gaze at Nicholas Devin Cocker, and whisper, "He's so pretty!"

With sweat dripping down his face, too, Jeremy grins, "He's handsome, baby, never call a boy pretty."

It wasn't an easy birth. Three hours in I screamed for drugs and Jeremy couldn't believe it. Neither could Cecily, since I'm a no pills type o' gal. But when she saw my face and heard me say, "Do I look like I'm kidding?" she went and got my doctor to shoot me up. My mom did it and she turned out okay. I mean I turned out okay. Did I mention I'm high?

"He's so pretty," I breathe again. "Pretty pretty pretty."

Jeremy starts laughing, saying to Cecily, "Tell your mom Meagan's stoned. I want to see how Lynne reacts."

"Oh, Mom was smoking when she was pregnant, she won't be shocked."

"Cess!" I cry out. "You're not supposed to say that."

She makes a face, pursing her lips. "Are you kidding? In the sixties they smoked in airplanes! There were ashtrays in the backseat of cars! God, they had ashtrays built into *hospital rooms*!!! Nobody knew it was bad for you."

"I wasn't born in the forties."

"Yeah, that's not the decade I said. She is high."

Jeremy chuckles. "You guys finished? We just had a son. I'd like to get back to the alien my wife is holding."

"I'm going to give you guys some time alone." Cecily heads off.

The doctor tells me, "I need to clean Nicholas up now. We'll swaddle him and bring him back to you in your room."

"Two more seconds," Jeremy tells her, not even glancing her way because he can't stop looking at our boy. "Just give us that."

Tiny, dark pink lips yawn as even tinier fingers stretch all the way out. Jeremy and I smile at each other, so tired and so happy, and his hand is stroking my gross hair. He loves me.

"We're not having another one. That was too hard to watch you go through, baby. I won't do that to you again."

Patiently I whisper, "We'll have at least ten more."

"What did you just say??"

"Okay, two. Maybe three. Two! One more. We'll see."

Itty-bitty fingers touch Jeremy's open palm and my husband's voice deepens as he speaks to his son. "Nicholas, I'm going to be your best friend, little man. When you reach out, my hand will always be there to grasp."

Something very special happened the day Nicholas was born. The ghosts from Jeremy's past that still lingered in his heart were quieted. His eyes cleared and his heart opened more than it had even with me, because Jeremy bonded to Nicholas more than with any of our future children, though of course he loved them all. I knew why he opened up. I could see how much Nicholas was like my Devin...our Devin. Nicholas became the funniest of the Cocker cousins, often making the whole family laugh with the crazy things he did. Jeremy asked me when Nicholas turned nine and had just shocked the whole family by streaking through his birthday party, "Do you think it's possible Devin came back to us?"

We'd never discussed reincarnation before, so I was surprised that my Marine would be open to such a fantastical (in the true meaning of the word) idea. But there he was, soberly asking me and hoping it was true.

I say on a smile, "I believe anything's possible. After all, Jeremy...I met you."

THE END.

The children of the six brothers will have their own love stories, next. I hope you enjoyed falling in love with Jake, Jett, Jaxson, Jason & Justin, and Jeremy, the one who made me cry.

Xx, Faleena Hopkins

NOTE FROM FALEENA

I just had to share some things about writing this story, because this one was pretty damn emotional for me.

And from what I've heard from my proofreaders, it was the most moving of the six brothers' stories for them, too.

Sure, it won't be like that for everyone.

We all have our own favorite brother. Mine might be Jaxson because I want to meet him in real life and be Rachel.

But Jeremy opened my heart in a whole different way. I have such indescribable respect for the people who serve our country that it took some doing to show up to the page knowing I had a responsibility. Turns out one of my proofreaders served our country as well, as did her husband, and was able to adjust one statement I'd made, so what a blessing that was. Also to have her stamp of approval.

First, an apology. I found out while researching that I should have named it, "Cocky Marine," because a Marine personally told me they never call themselves soldiers. "No, only Marines!" To say I was dismayed is an understatement, because unfortunately by that time the cover was already everywhere, the preorder was live with over 2000 sold by that time, and couldn't be changed. To make up for it, I never use the word soldier in the actual book.

My dad was in the Navy and nearly died two times in submarines while miles below sea level in enemy waters. We say, in my family, that he is like a cat and now has only four lives left, since he was also a police officer for 27 years, with some long, incredible stories I won't go into here. So, I went into this tale struggling.

I wanted to not just write a romance, but a true-to-life tale that honors them. Even though Jeremy is a Cocker, confident as a man, he is not immune. He will try to 'handle it' on his own, as so many people do, and he will in the end need help, just like we all do. Someone who maybe even unwittingly provides a way out, like Meagan's explosion into his life. Luckily humor warmed both their cold hearts, and they were able to save each other through absolutely no planning of their own. It was sort of by accident. A car accident. Oy, sorry. As I was typing, that came out... ;)

The thing that's hard for me when I sit down is I never know how a story will go or end. I don't write outlines and I don't pre-plan plot. I 'write into the dark' as an author friend puts it. I'm not the only author who does this. I know a few. And Stephen King writes this way. Sit down with a character and a situation and see where they take you, that's how we roll. It's exciting to stay in suspense, because that keeps my readers in suspense with me, I like to believe. Plus if I already know the story, why write it?

But it makes for some nail-biting tension before I sit down. Like life, you just never know what's going to come up and how you'll deal with it. I laughed a lot with these two characters and cried like a baby, as well.

Anyway, maybe it's because it's the last of the Cocker Brothers that I felt so damn much. I love this family.

If I made you laugh, yay! If I made you cry, sorry…but yay! If I didn't, I'll try harder the next book. Kidding. I have no idea what Hannah's book will be like. We'll find out together. But I have a feeling she's a wild child who will take us all on a very fun ride.

And if you read all of what I just wrote, I'm humbled and honored. Did it even make sense? I rambled a bit…but hey, it's my personal note, so I get to be a little messy, right? I need more coffee.

Love and light…

Xx, Faleena Hopkins

P.S. My proofers didn't read this note. If there are typos, that's all me. And p.s. If you ever find a typo and want to write to me, please do. I always love the help. Faleena@faleenahopkins.com

Faleena Hopkins

COCKER BROTHERS SERIES NOTE

I decided to write bonus chapters for this entire series, scenes that take place years after each book ends so you can experience what happens to these wonderful characters later. For Cocky Roomie, we get to meet their three children. Cocky Cowboy, we get to meet Ben. They're very fun, include more sexy scenes, and can only be accessed by eBook downloads at this time, when you sign up for private club's newsletter. The Kindle app is free for any device, and I also offer Epubs and PDFs.

You can access these through the signup button on my FB Page:

http://facebook.com/authorfaleenahopkins

Enjoy!
Xx, Faleena Hopkins

Faleena Hopkins

TO GET IN TOUCH:

www. AuthorFaleenaHopkins.com

http://facebook.com/authorfaleenahopkins
(mailing list link is there under: Signup)

Twitter and Instagram: @faleenahopkins

Pinterest: FaleenaMHopkins
(there is a board dedicated to this series)

To learn more about my acting/filmmaking career:
http://imdb.me/faleenahopkins

BY FALEENA HOPKINS

Cocky Roomie
Cocky Biker
Cocky Cowboy
Cocky Romantic
Cocky Senator
Cocky Soldier
A Honey Badger X-Mas (from Cocky Biker)
Cocky Senator's Daughter: Hannah.

You Don't Know Me

Anything For You Series:
Changing For You
Reaching For You
Searching For You

Werewolves Of Chicago: Curragh
Werewolves Of Chicago: Howard
Werewolves Of Chicago: Xavier

Werewolves Of New York: Nathaniel
Werewolves Of New York: Eli
Werewolves Of New York: Darik
Werewolves Of New York: Dontae

Faleena Hopkins

ABOUT THE AUTHOR

Faleena Hopkins published her first novel in May of 2013 and due to the warm reception of her stories, was able to quit her day-job as a professional portrait photographer by September of that year to write full time.

A California native and a Los Angeles resident for twenty-three years, she moved to Atlanta, GA in December 2015 to write love stories and prepare filming for her first independent feature film. This is where the Cocker Brothers series was inspired.

Also an actress for over twenty years, her work has been praised in reviews by the Los Angeles Times, Variety and Hollywood Reporter and she intends to direct and star in her first movie, to keep pushing the boundaries of what people say she can and cannot do.

The bracelet she wears every day bears the engraving: *She believed she could so she did.* Inspiring others to follow their dreams is a big part of her passion and she regularly helps authors self-publish their way to success by sharing how she was able to get where she is, and the mistakes she navigated along the way.

Made in the USA
Middletown, DE
01 February 2018